Otherworld Origins ~ Book 1

I0626666

Awakened

Julie Scholfield

Silver Book Press

DEDICATION

To my family and friends that have encouraged me on this journey.
Your love and support has been a blessing.

CONTENTS

PROLOGUE

Trieva

The fog encircles the bay like a dark blanket. The air was cool, and the moisture from the fog makes it feel even cooler. I wrap my jacket tighter around me. I wish I had worn something just a bit heavier. Lombard Street still had plenty of traffic going through it, even this late at night. I am not sure where I am going only that I am trying to find out what has been making me so uneasy lately.

For months I have felt as if my people have started to gather in San Francisco, only none of them bothered to contact me. I have tried to locate them only to feel as if I am following ghosts. Why would the Sidhe be here? I have never felt this many of my own people since before I entered the changeling program over thirty five years ago.

I make my way past Broderick Street and can feel the pull of the Sidhe but it is weak. Again, it feels as if I am following the pull of ghosts. It makes me feel uneasy and I shiver. I begin to feel the pull from the north, towards the docks. The wind picks up bringing the strong briny smell of the ocean. My curly strawberry blonde hair whips around my face making it even harder to see.

I know I am near the Palace of Fine Arts even though I can't see its dome. The pull is getting stronger as I continue towards the docks. The street lights are more spread out as I cut north on Baker Street. There is barely any light as the fog and cloud cover blocks out the moon and the stars. I feel a very sharp pull to the west. It is coming from the Palace of Fine Arts.

The parking lot lights are not lit as there is no performance scheduled for tonight. For some reason I can feel a mass of people nearby. I walk along and I suddenly realize there is no noise other than my own feet crunching on the grass. The animals that usually call this place home are too quiet. It is then, that I smell an increasing aroma of copper pennies.

My eyes widen in alarm, my breath starts to quicken. The scent of blood is in the air. I was so involved in my own thoughts and following the pull, I wasn't paying attention to my surroundings. I curse under my breath. A tall blonde man comes out from the bushes behind me near the building.

"You do not belong here, Sidhe. Your intrusion will cost you".

"Who are you to say I do not belong? What are you doing here? Why are there so many gathering in once place?"

"Spying on us will not gain the Sidhe the upper hand, you will soon know our vengeance!"

"Spying? I don't understand."

"It doesn't matter, you are not long for this world."

The man lunges at me and I quickly dodge his first strike, barely missing the small curved blade he holds in his left hand. I am not prepared for confrontation, let alone combat. It has been thirty five years since I last sparred with anyone, but it was only practice during my training for the program. It is obvious the man knows I am Sidhe, like him, but how can he not know who I am?

The man springs again only this time I am not able to get out of the way quick enough and he slices through my jacket and into my back. I cry out in pain, it hurts too much to be silent like I have been trained. If I do not get my act together, this is not going to end well. There is movement to my right, more people start moving in my direction. It is in that moment that I found the "ghosts" as I call them. Only they aren't ghosts, they are barely even Sidhe!

The distraction and my piss poor planning for not being prepared cost me everything. The blonde man slid his blade through my ribs and up into my heart. His breath hot on my face as he gloats in satisfaction.

"The high court and all the Sidhe of the Seelie and Unseelie courts shall feel the same. Things will soon be better. Everything will change under Morcant's rule."

I have no idea what he is talking about. All I know is that those I love are in great danger. The blonde man spits in my face before walking off not even bothering to make sure that my crumpled body on the grass had actually perished. I try to think but it is so hard. How can I tell my husband and my children that I love them? I can't breathe and the pull of the darkness is overwhelming. I manage to grab my sigil and mentally call for help. Then the darkness came.

CHAPTER 1

Avalon

I look around me but all I can see is darkness. The place smells of damp earth and I can hear what sounds like water dripping into a puddle. The air is frigid and makes me wish I had more than just a flimsy t-shirt on.

"Hello?"

The place seems to echo like a cavern, bouncing my voice around. I feel around me. All I feel is hard ground made of dirt and rocks. I am alone and begin to feel really creeped out. A slight whispering sound seems to be coming from all around me. I can't make out what is being said. Hands grab me and start dragging me in the darkness.

I try to grab ahold of anything to stop my momentum, to fight being pulled in a direction by an unknown figure. It was an epic fail, I keep getting pulled. The figure stops dragging me and lifts me up onto something before releasing his grip.

The area is slowly starting to brighten by a faint silvery light. I now see that I am in some sort of large cavern, like the ones I saw in Carlsbad, NM, while on a family vacation. The stalactites look like long bony fingers reaching toward the ground. I am on some sort of raised platform, almost like a stage.

I look toward the source of the light and see the most amazing man I have ever laid eyes on. He seems too perfect, like he isn't even human. He has sandy blonde hair, built like a runner, and has the most unusual eye color; yellow, green, and around the pupil is silver. He looks at me with worry on his face, but also like he is waiting for me to do something.

I start to move toward him when an ice cold hand clamps down on my wrist, preventing me from going anywhere. The cavern grows dark again and I can't see who has me now. There is a sharp poke on my finger and I know it was enough to draw blood. The cavern starts to smell like copper pennies.

Something hard clamps around my neck and the pain is too much. It is hard to breathe, I am being held in place and I can't move an inch. Slowly the darkness becomes all-consuming and I am scared.

The sound of my phone going off wakes me up, I realize I am once again safe in my room. I feel like an ice cube, so I rub my neck and my arms to warm up.

"I hate that damn dream." I mutter to myself.

I look around my room to reassure myself that I am not in that dark hole. The sun is filtering through the mini blinds and the sheer white curtains in my room. My sparse furnishings look like any normal young adult's room. The only decoration in my room is the two year old photograph on my nightstand of my family. It echoes of when times were better and my mom was alive.

I try to shake myself of the melancholy that tries to take ahold of me whenever I look at that photo. I pick up my phone to turn off the alarm that is still ringing and notice the time.

"Shit! I'm going to be late!"

I grab some laundry that is sitting on top of my desk and run to the bathroom. The last thing I need is to be late again. It would be the third time in less than two weeks. I've only been working at CommTech for a few months. My first and only job since moving to Colorado last year.

I flip on the lights and turn on the shower. The brightness of the stark white room and the strong smell of bleach hits me. I groan and hop into the shower which hasn't had time to warm up yet. Thank God it isn't winter or I would have frozen my butt off. I quickly wash my hair and body and jump out of the shower.

After putting on the clothes, I dry off my hair with the towel. I quickly put my hair up in a loose ponytail with an old scrunchie. I already know that my hair will fall out of it before long anyway. I glance at myself in the mirror and I'm pleasantly surprised. My messy straight brown hair actually looks half decent and my clothes match. Even the odd red highlights that I have look exceptionally spunky today. I open the drawer and put on some mascara and a swipe of baby pink lip gloss and leave the room.

I'm so glad there are no important meetings to attend today at work that makes it necessary to dress up slightly. My purple t-shirt, jeans, and Birkenstocks are normal, late summer-time wear. I pick up my phone where I had left it on the bed and start to put it in my pocket when it rings. I look down at the caller ID, its Tripp. I answer the phone.

"Hey Tripp."

"Hey yourself. Did you wake up late again and forget something?" Tripp snaps.

"Well I did wake up late, but I don't think I forgot anything." I reply honestly.

"Oh I see how I rate now." Tripp teases.

"Huh?" I'm totally confused.

"We had plans for coffee this morning chica!" Tripp raises his voice.

"Oh crap, I'm so sorry!"

"Don't worry about it, I picked up your usual and I'll bring it with me to work, see you there." Tripp laughs at me.

"Thanks Tripp, you're the best!" Coffee! Just what I needed.

"Yeah, I know. See ya." Tripp chuckles as he hangs up.

I click off my phone and put it in my purse. I walk through the door and lock it on my way out. I'm going to owe him big for standing him up for the second time this week. These nightmares I have been having since June on my 18th birthday, are starting to get beyond ridiculous. They are always the same, they never change, and I can never control them. When I wake up, I'm a nervous wreck the rest of the day. I'm becoming a mess!

CHAPTER 2

Melanie

The lobby of the office seems bright today. The natural light shines through the glass wall of the building. White square columns break up the glass wall to give it some support. There are several other people milling about the lobby but I don't know if they are here for the same reason I am.

Brittany and Michelle are busy with their faces in their phones as usual. I'm waiting to see what the new supervisor looks like, since his first day is today. Today was definitely not like any other day, there is a different feeling in the air, or maybe I'm over excited for some reason.

The door opens and the most gorgeous specimen of man-flesh ever, walks into the lobby. It has to be him, Nickolai Savin, the new supervisor. I sigh. He looks to be about six foot three, with bronze skin, brown hair and bright grey-green eyes. His body is built like a star quarterback with a broad chest and shoulders that taper down to a slim waist. I vow to myself that he will be mine.

I spot Avalon and Tripp coming into the building talking together, joined at the hip with their Starbucks in hand, as usual. Neither one is paying attention to what is going on outside of their bubble. One would think they were dating if you didn't know that Tripp was undeniably gay. The little idiot is going to walk right into Nickolai! She will probably dump her coffee all over him no doubt.

"Watch where you're going!" I call out.

It's too late. Avalon walks right into the back of Nickolai. Instead of dumping it on him though, her coffee cup goes flying but oddly enough ends up landing on the floor right side up without a drop being spilled. My eyes widen in surprise. I look around and no one else has noticed how the coffee cup landed so perfectly. I glance back at Nickolai. I catch a glimpse at Avalon's face and the look that briefly crosses her face makes me believe she knows about the odd way the cup landed, as if it was no weird, freak occurrence. There was always something odd about her and this was just another one of those things to solidify it.

"Oh my gosh! I'm so sorry! Are you alright?" Avalon asks Nickolai.

I bend down to pick up his briefcase that he had dropped when the clumsy oaf walked into him. Oh, a part of me wished I had bumped into him like that, full body contact. The thought makes my whole body tingle.

"Clumsy idiot." I mutter.

I look up and Nickolai has his hands on the sides of Avalon's arms.

"You can bump into me any day." Nickolai smiles at Avalon, a dimple appears on his left cheek. Avalon blushes but smiles back at him.

I come up beside them to make my presence known and hand Nickolai his briefcase, trying to block Avalon from view.

"Thanks." He says quickly.

He leans down near my face. I'm not sure what he's about to do, it makes me nervous and excited, all at the same time.

"Next time you should keep your thoughts in your head instead of blurting them out like that."

His whispered suggestion tickles my neck, the smell of mint from his mouth lingers in the air. Crap! Strike one, Mel. Smooth, real smooth. I berate myself as I watch Nickolai join Avalon and Tripp as they walk down the hall. Brittany and Michelle walk up behind me, finally bringing their noses out of their phones.

"Strike two for Avalon." They both say in unison.

"The nerve of her stealing your moment!" Brittany exclaims.

It makes me feel better knowing that my girls have my back, but I'm getting angrier by the moment. I cross my arms and watch the three of them walk down the hall, laughing and talking as if they have always known each other. Somehow, I need to change Nickolai's first impression of me, but I'm not sure how to do it. As for Avalon, there is something about her I just don't like.

Avalon has always rubbed me wrong, but it isn't something I can explain, just a feeling. Maybe it is jealousy, not that I will admit that to anyone. Avalon is one of those girls that is beyond beautiful and doesn't seem to know it. The kind that always look like they woke up perfect. She probably could have been a model if she wasn't so short. Her small little body is thin and perfect for such a petite frame. Avalon's dark brown hair is straight but almost seemed to be perfectly styled even in a messy up-do like she was sporting today. How did she do that?

It's not as if I'm ugly or anything. I'm pretty tall, almost six foot. I'm also thin but well-toned from years of dancing. My fair complexion and fiery, out-of-control, red hair takes a lot more work in the mornings to be even slightly presentable. Plus, I would rather be dead than wear the clothes that Avalon does; the old t-shirts, jeans and clunky Birkenstocks. It just isn't fair that she waltzes in, makes a clumsy fool of herself, and then gets the guy too. I shake my head. No, that is not going to happen.

CHAPTER 3

Avalon

So after completely embarrassing myself in front of the new supervisor, he decides to walk with us to the cubicle farm. Why can't I just suffer my embarrassment privately? Nickolai, Tripp, and I walk into the hallway. The buzz of a hive of people on the phone fills the air. Cubicles line the hallway and are sectioned off into pods of thirteen.

I try to keep up with Nickolai and Tripp. Their legs are long compared to my really short ones. I sip my coffee in silence. Tripp doesn't seem to mind the extra company. I already know he wants to get to know the new supervisor. He is such a suck-up. I just hope no one noticed how my coffee landed or the look on my face when it landed exactly how I wanted it to. I don't want to be labeled a freak. Especially since this is not the first time something like this has happened. Tripp strikes up a conversation with Nickolai, bringing me out of my self-absorbed thoughts.

"So, where are you from Nickolai? With that righteous tan, you can't be from around here. What's your story?" Tripp asks.

Nickolai laughs and looks at Tripp.

"Actually I am from here. I was born and raised in Eaton. From the words you're using you don't sound like you're from here. SoCal?" Nickolai says.

"Whoa, yeah. You've been there?" Tripp seems impressed that Nickolai can tell he is from California with his blatant Cali-lingo.

I try not to laugh at the obviousness of it.

"A few times, when I was in the Military. I just got out a few months ago, saw the job opportunity posted on the company website. When I saw that it was available close to home, I went for it."

"Military? Man, gotta love a man in uniform!" Tripp quips.

"Erm." Nickolai shifts a bit uncomfortably.

Tripp laughs.

"I know you don't swing my way bro. I'm just teasing and getting Avalon all pink again." Tripp grins at me with an impish look.

I blush again giving away everything. I can't stop looking at the man. I have never acted this way before around guys, but it is like a pull with him. His slightly wavy brown hair has natural blond highlights in it. His chiseled features match what one might think a military man should look like. He definitely isn't a flabby or lazy man; far from it.

"So since I am new here and don't know anyone, would you care to join me for lunch Avalon?" Nickolai looks directly at me.

I swallow hard. I wasn't expecting this.

"Well I always eat lunch with Tripp, and I would hate to abandon him." I say.

I see the hopeful look on Nickolai's face start to fall and I suddenly feel the need to invite him along.

"You can join us if you like. I would like to know more about your adventures in the military." I add.

He smiles at me. His full lips part to show his bright white, perfect teeth. A dimple appears on his left cheek. I could get lost in that face all day.

"Well this is my stop, I'll see you two at lunch."

Nickolai walks over to the empty supervisor desk and starts opening his briefcase. He looks up and catches me staring at him. He smiles and waves at me. I turn red again at being caught. I feel like such a dork. Tripp laughs.

"I have never seen you act like that before. It was quite entertaining."

"Oh shut up."

"That's one nice butt he's got."

"Tripp! Seriously! I know he has a nice butt but I don't need you talking about it." I can feel my face getting redder by the minute.

Tripp laughs harder.

"Lunch is going to be fun." Tripp grins at me and makes a funny face.

I do the only thing I can at work. I stick my tongue out at him like a five year old and walk away.

~*~

Finally, lunchtime arrives. I haven't been able to think of anything else since I invited Nickolai for lunch. I really did want to get to know him better, but I didn't want to look desperate. I catch Tripp as he is walking away from his team, heading toward mine and we walk together towards Nickolai.

Nickolai is sitting at his desk, facing his computer with his phone to his face. He is pinching the bridge of his nose with his left thumb and index finger. Tripp snickers. I look at him knowingly. A difficult customer that doesn't understand the policies we have to follow.

I have no idea how much longer he will be on the phone so I grab his blue sticky note pad, leaving a note that we will be grabbing lunch in the café and will be sitting outside in the quad at the umbrella covered tables. Nickolai notices the note and looks up, smiling warmly at me. He glances at the note and mouths that he will join us as soon as he can. I nod. Tripp and I head off toward the café.

Various food selections are available at the café, with stainless steel counters that separated the customers from the food prep area. I look over the menu of today's offerings trying to find something safe. I didn't want a piece of salad stuck in my teeth while I was having lunch with Nickolai, so salads and wraps are out. I hate peperoni pizza and there is sausage being served for the entrée, double yuck. I decide on a cheese quesadilla, it's safe and doesn't look like I would be shoving half a cooked cow in my mouth, like I would if I ordered a cheeseburger.

Tripp and I walk up to the grill, I order my quesadilla and move over to the side.

"I would like a cheeseburger, with Pepper Jack, hold the onions, medium rare and fresh fries not the stuff that's been sitting under that pathetic warmer that makes them taste like rubber." Tripp moves over and stands next to me.

I hold back a snicker. To others he sounds so rude, but he has the tendency to be too blunt. We wait for our order when I feel a pair of hands cover my eyes. I'm almost in a slight panic when Tripp ruins the suspense.

"Hey Nickolai, we wondered if you were going to get off that nasty call before our lunch was over."

"Well not everyone understands the word no, sometimes they have to have it told to them in various ways before they get a clue that the answer won't change."

Tripp laughs.

I smile at Nickolai. "I am glad you could make it."

"I am too. I'm starving, but I will not miss lunch with you if I can help it." Nickolai grins at me.

The lights seem suddenly way too bright in here, like I'm in a spot light that I don't want to be in. Nickolai orders his lunch and waits with us. Our orders are up fairly quickly, which we grab and head to the cashier. I put mine up and get out my debit card.

"Her lunch is on me, don't take her card, please."

I look at Nickolai in surprise, I wasn't expecting that.

"Thank you. You don't have to you know, I can pay for my own lunch."

"I know I don't have to, I want to."

As Nickolai is talking to me with the smile that lights up his whole face, the warm sensation fills my body again. As the cashier rings up the total, Tripp comes up to the counter with his order, along with chips, a candy bar and a Dr. Pepper. Usual Tripp, 2,000 calories in one meal. We wait for Tripp to pay for his lunch before heading outside.

The sun shines bright. The reflection off the plastic umbrellas over the tables is blinding. I spot an empty, mostly clean table and head over, knowing the guys will follow. Tripp immediately pulls out a wet nap out of his pocket and wipes down the table. The guy does not like anything to be unsanitary, heaven forbid he eats at a dirty table. I smile at the thought

"Penny for your thoughts?" Nickolai smiles at me.

"Oh my thoughts are worth more than a penny." I tease.

Tripp snorts.

"Knowing Avalon, she is probably having a small laugh to herself at my expense and my fear of uncleanliness." Tripp waves his hand to everything around us.

"Not the outdoors type?"

I almost snort at the thought of Tripp camping.

"Hell no! Give me a nice temperature controlled room with Wi-Fi, TV and music and I'm set, at least until I get hungry."

"Yeah. That will last what, an hour?" I grin at Tripp, knowing his insatiable hunger.

Nickolai smiles and bites into his burger. Tripp follows suit. I pick at the quesadilla in front of me.

"Not hungry?" Nickolai looks at me.

"Ha! She is just worried that if she eats in front of you, she will get something stuck in her teeth or if she chows down like us, you will think she eats like a pig."

"That is so not it and you know it Tripp!" I push his burger in his face with an impish grin. He is totally spot on but I can't let

Nickolai know that. It sounds silly the way Tripp explains it. "I'm just…"

Before I can say anything else, Melanie and her group of clones walk up and scoot another table next to ours so that she can sit by Nickolai. Melanie, Brittany and Michelle all sit down in unison, all three also have the cheese quesadilla. I want to hide, as my choice in lunch is now so very obvious.

"Avalon, I want to apologize for earlier today. I was upset about something at home and took it out on you, I hope you will forgive me." Melanie looks at me apologetically.

Well this is new. Melanie being nice to me. That never happens. Ever since I started working here she has been a thorn in my side. More than likely she is trying to look better in front of Nickolai, doing damage control on her first impression this morning.

"Apology accepted. Everyone has bad days." I smile nonchalantly back at her.

"So Nickolai, I heard you were in the military? Which branch?" Melanie turns her attention to the real person she and her clones came here for. Melanie scoots closer to Nickolai and puts her hand on his shoulder. She looks like she would have wrapped herself all over him if we were not here.

"Navy." Nickolai manages to get out between bites.

"Nick! I didn't know you worked here?" A voice calls out.

"Drew! Long time bud. How have you been man?" Nickolai waves to guy walking up the path towards us.

Drew walks up and stands next to the table. His stocky, muscular frame would block out the sun if he was a few inches taller. He rubs his hand back and forth over his buzzed head, the dark hair just a whisper on his scalp. He reminds me of some of the guys from my old high school wrestling team. His bright blue eyes gaze around the table, a smile appears on his face as he notices Melanie, but starts to fade as he notices her body language.

"I just started today. Saw the position available for a supervisor here, and longed to come back home. How long have you been here?" Nickolai looks up at Drew.

"I've been here just over a year. I sit right behind Avalon. She will surprise you, all quiet when you first meet her, then she never shuts up once she gets to know you." Drew teases me.

I grin, Tripp snorts and Melanie snickers.

"Good. I like a girl that participates in a conversation, it means I don't have to carry it all by myself."

There is a slight flash in Nickolai's eyes after that and he is looking right at me. It's starting to get warmer and I hope my face isn't growing pink. His gaze is so intense it makes me a bit uneasy, but it isn't unpleasant.

Tripp snickers and I look at him to see if he will clue me in. He looks at me, glances quickly at Melanie, and looks back at his burger. I glance over at Melanie, her hand is off Nickolai's shoulder. She looks like she is thinking hard about something and has a look of annoyance on her face as she picks at her quesadilla.

"Drew, there is an extra chair here, you could sit down you know." I gesture to the empty chair next to Nickolai.

Drew smiles and sits down.

"I didn't want to intrude on a lunch gathering I wasn't invited to."

At that, Melanie glares at Drew. Drew looks back at her and waggles his eyebrows at her. I'm trying so hard not to laugh, I quickly pick up my water bottle and start drinking. I watch Nickolai and Drew as they catch up with each other.

The alarm on my phone goes off signaling the end of our lunch break. Tripp and I excuse ourselves and start to head to the trash cans to get rid of the Styrofoam containers. A light touch on my arm stops me mid-stride and I turn.

"I know you have to get back to work, but is there any chance that we can go out for dinner sometime, just you and me?" Nickolai takes my hand waiting for a response.

The hopeful look in Nickolai's face is enough to make me want to melt into a puddle right there. The question, however, makes me nervous and anxious. I feel my heartbeat start to speed up and my hands start to get sweaty. Why not? What have I got to lose? Just my heart, which feels like it is still just starting to mend. I decide to take the chance.

"Sure. How about tonight?"

Nickolai smiles. "Pick you up at seven?"

"Um. How about I meet you there at seven?" I ask apprehensively.

"That will work," Nickolai replies.

"Where do you want to go so I dress appropriately?"

"Let's go to HuHot. It's nothing too fancy, just wear what's comfortable."

"Okay. I've never been there before. I'll see you later tonight." I try to keep it cool but I know I'm blushing when I smile back at him and squeeze his hand good-bye.

Tripp and I head back to the building. I turn to look back at Nickolai, who is sitting back down at the table, before I go inside. Drew is sitting in my vacated spot next to Michelle, and Melanie is back to hanging on Nickolai. The fact that he hasn't removed her hands from him, irks me to no end. I want to go back there and rip her off him and beat her up. The animosity in the thought startles me. I have never been a violent person nor a possessive person before. Tripp tugs on my arm and I follow him inside.

CHAPTER 4

Nickolai

I get to HuHot a little early. I want to be here when Avalon arrives. I find it funny that she did not want me to pick her up, but to meet her for dinner instead. I guess I can understand her cautiousness, but it still seems a little weird. A slight breeze is blowing and even outside the restaurant you can still smell the food and sauces in the air. My mouth starts to water slightly in anticipation. The streets are beginning to get fairly crowded with people since college is back in session.

HuHot, being a college age hang out, I figured it would be the most comfortable. Especially since she said she has not been here before. I give myself the once over again just to make sure I am moderately presentable. My faded blue Broncos t-shirt is clean but well worn, my jeans have some wear in them but no holes in awkward spots and my hiking boots have seen better days. I shrug. Well, at least I fit in with the usual crowd here.

I spot Avalon as she is walking toward me just as she steps onto the block. She must have parked at the parking garage two blocks down. Her dark hair gets caught in the breeze and the last rays of the sun hits the red highlights in her hair. She is wearing a faded orange Broncos t-shirt, jeans and dress boots. The fact that we dressed so similar without planning it makes me want to laugh.

As she approaches she notices my clothing and starts to laugh. Her laugh is light and musical and changes her entire face into one of enjoyment. I smile at her.

"You'd think we planned this!" She was still giggling a little.

"Yeah, well, you have great taste. Great minds, you know." I quip.

I usher her inside with my hand on the small of her back and she doesn't shy away from my touch. The scent of her is overwhelming to me and drowns out the scent of the restaurant. Cherry blossoms and strawberries. It becomes my favorite scent in the world in an instant. We wait to be seated in the crowded restaurant and she holds onto my hand. It fits so perfectly in mine. My mind wanders a bit at the feel of her.

We are led to the table by the waitress and I explain to her how everything works. I lead her over to the food stations and start filling the bowls with various meat, noodles and veggies. I don't even get a chance to start explaining the sauces when she is already applying them to her bowls. The sauces she is using are quite spicy. I look at her, wondering if she knows what she is doing.

"We had something similar where I grew up in

California." She grins when she notices me looking at her warily.

We line up behind the other waiting guests and watch the cooks on the round grill. I enjoy the closeness of her as she leans against me in line. She is so small and delicate, I just want to protect her from everything. Once the cooks get done we head back with our full plates back to the table, where our drinks and rice are waiting.

"So you grew up in California?" I ask her.

"Yep, San Francisco to be exact. I'm still trying to get used to the seasonal weather changes here," she confesses.

"When did you move to Colorado?"

"Last year, right before my senior year in high school," she says.

I hadn't thought she might not be eighteen yet. Crap. It is workable but I was hoping she was at least eighteen, girls were always so hard to judge.

"So tell me more about you Nickolai? What do you like to do? How old you are? That sort of thing."

"Well I grew up in Eaton, Colorado. I'll be twenty-three in November. I like to do anything outdoors; hunt, fish, hike and camping. Obviously I like watching football." I pull a bit on my shirt. "I didn't peg you for a football fan, least of all the Denver Broncos."

She giggled. "Well as for the Denver Broncos, I was never really into football before we moved but I started watching it with my dad last year to spend time with him. He hasn't been the same since my mom died." Her face darkens as she finishes speaking.

"Oh, I'm sorry to hear. How long has it been since she passed away?"

"Almost two years. My dad has been pretty withdrawn and secludes himself in his art room to paint. At least that is what he says. My mom, she didn't pass away. She was killed. It is all some big mystery. The police told my dad that there were no clues left behind to find out who did this to my mom, so whoever did it has gotten away with it." The anger drips from her voice, like someone had just ripped a Band-Aid off a wound that had not healed yet.

"I'm so sorry I brought this up, I can see that you're still hurting from this. I didn't want to cause you any grief or discomfort." I take hold of her clenched hand and squeeze.

She looks up at me from the table, her eyes shining with unshed tears. Crap! I'm batting a thousand with this girl! She smiles tentatively back at me and nods her head.

"It's ok. The silliest thing can bring up those memories, and it's not your fault in the least." She shrugs it off and the look on her face changes. "So onto other topics, my birthday is in June, I just turned eighteen."

A look of relief must have passed on my face or something because she snickers in response.

"I like to draw, paint and swim. I have gone tent camping once but would be open to do so again if I had the chance." She smiles playfully.

"Out with the bugs and the dirt! No thanks!" A voice

says off to my right.

The sound of that voice is startling. I turn my head to see Melanie standing next to the short wall that separates the dining area from the grill area. She looks at Avalon with a look of disgust on her face that quickly vanishes as she sees that I'm looking at her. She turns to me with a smile, and it was a beautiful smile, but the smile did not quite reach her eyes. The look in her eyes reminded me of a predator hunting their prey. It gives me a cold shiver.

"Do you mind if we go? I'm suddenly not hungry anymore," Avalon says.

I look at Avalon who looks like she just wants to be invisible than cause a scene or deal with Melanie. "Sure, I think I'm done as well, let me walk you to your car." I lay down cash on the table to cover the check and help Avalon into her jacket, leaving Melanie to gape at us as we leave the restaurant.

The street lamps illuminate the walks. The sidewalks are crowded with people. A cool breeze wafts the scent of cherry blossoms and strawberries back in my face. I don't think I will ever tire of that smell. I breathe in deeply and take Avalon's hand in mine as we walk down the block towards her car.

I park the car in the parking lot of Martinez Park and lock the doors. The wind has picked up but it will make this run enjoyable. I pass by the park area and notice a man sitting at one of the tables alone. Why he is here at this late hour is none of my business, I just need to release all this pent up frustration inside me, before I lose control. I hope tonight's date went as well as I hope it did but it's hard to tell.

I feel like I was stepping on eggshells at times with her. It was very confusing, one minute she is sad, then angry, then acts like nothing is bothering her. I can understand the sad then angry emotions about her mom's murder, but to be able to switch it off, is something I have rarely seen anyone do before. I only know of one that can do that and Morcant is not someone I would want to compare Avalon to.

Being back in familiar surroundings is great after so many years away from it. The cool air is clean and fresh. I can smell the animals at the nearby farm but it isn't an unpleasant smell. The whisper of the leaves in the trees from the breeze reminds me of a time when I was a kid running along this trail.

I walk farther on the Poudre Trail to get out of sight from the man in the park and people in their apartments and houses. I look around to make sure I am well out of view. There is no lighting on this part of the trail, which is good because not everyone would be able to accept what they saw next. I focus on my hidden self, the source of my pent up frustration, and release it.

The air shimmers and my perception shifts. My body is closer to the ground and all around me is varying degrees of grey. I stretch my muscles, I can feel my tail thumping slightly on the trail. The breeze ruffles the striped fur on my body and I scent the air. No one is around, and good thing. I don't think anyone would be prepared to run into a tiger in the darkness. I chuckle to myself thinking about how someone would react. The beast within wants to run and not think anymore. It's time to relax. It's time to run.

CHAPTER 5

Avalon

I wake up from a peaceful sleep and stretch my limbs slowly in enjoyment. It is the first night in a week that I didn't have that horrid dream. The date with Nickolai went well, at least I think it did. I really need to keep my anger and memories in check though. I hope I didn't put him off. Then again, he never asked for a second date. I start to worry that I made a very bad impression.

The memory of Melanie eavesdropping on our conversation starts to piss me off. Is she following him? First, she shows up at our lunch. That I could understand since we were at work and he asked to join us in front of her. Showing up at HuHot during our date and eavesdropping was a bit much. I guess I can give her a pass since she has been nice to me lately. Being gracious and letting it drop where Nickolai was concerned was starting to rub me the wrong way.

In the course of my inner musings I notice movement

out of the corner of my eye, I turn my head to look, but nothing is there. The movement looked like a figure walking from one side of my room to the other. It was silvery, pale and very tall. I did not need to be seeing ghosts on top of everything else in my life, though this is definitely not the first time I've seen something like this. It's been happening all my life.

Odd things always seems to happen. Well, odd in being that most people did not experience these things. Stories my dad told me about when I was growing up, that I thought were just dreams, actually happened. For instance, when I was seven, I swam with seals and their pups at the Children's Beach in San Diego. Another, when I was three, sitting at the bottom of a public pool listening and watching people.

Other things I actually do remember. My family going to a Marine park, they had lost track of me, and when they found me, I was sitting at the observation window talking to one of the dolphins. I remember it was performing tricks and blowing bubble rings when I asked it to. I was so engrossed I had never realized that my parents were looking for me.

Another instance, was my friend, Una. She was so pretty. She was tall, with long golden hair, fair skin, blue-green eyes and a silver gown that sparkled like it was encrusted with diamonds. She always came to me when I would go on nature walks outside of the city, when I had stopped to rest or eat lunch, she would just show up. I never thought about how uncanny it was that she just happened to keep popping up out of nowhere. No one else ever saw her and when I described her to my parents once they looked at me in shock, but treated Una like an imaginary friend.

No. I certainly didn't need any more weirdness, nor did

I want to see the ghosts today.

~*~

The smell of a variety of aromas along with the usual espresso permeates through the coffee shop. Pastries and scones are on display behind glass at the counter, tempting everyone who orders. The walls are covered in a mocha colored paint, with small accents of red and gold. The lighting is low and comforting. I sit down in the plush gold chair next to Tripp with my caramel macchiato in hand.

"So how was it last night?" Tripp looks at me inquisitively, sitting on the edge of his seat hoping to get juicy details.

"It was good. I think." I bit my lip.

"You think? What happened?" Tripp shifts in his chair tucking one leg underneath him.

"Well it was going good, the chemistry was definitely there. Something happened when we were talking and it reminded me of my mom. I got angry. Not at him of course, just angry."

Tripp shifts a bit in his seat. "Well how did he handle that?"

"Pretty well actually, since I realized what I was doing and switched topics abruptly. I just hope he wasn't paying too close attention to that so he doesn't think I'm a total nut job."

"So what else happened? I'm sure he doesn't think you're a total nut job. Did he ask you for another date?"

"You won't believe this. Melanie showed up and

eavesdropped on our conversation!"

Tripp snorts. "You're kidding!"

"Totally serious! She even commented on what we were talking about. That is the only way I knew she was there! I wanted to slap her."

"First our lunch yesterday, and then she was at the restaurant you guys went to too? What is she a stalker? Where did you go for dinner?"

"I know right! We went to HuHot because I told him I had never been there before."

"Well since I didn't get a call to go pick you up at the police station, I assume there was no assault on the vile woman?"

I giggle. "No, but suddenly I didn't want to eat and I wanted to leave. He agreed, left cash on the table to cover our bill and we walked out."

Tripp whistles. "Impressive and classy. You didn't say anything to her?"

"Nope, we both ignored her and left. He walked me to my car, kissed me and said good night. He didn't ask for another date though, is that bad?"

"Hard to tell, he did kiss you. Maybe he is letting the thought of him consume you!" Tripp teases.

"Oh shut up!" I laugh and smack him in the arm. "It's time to go or we will be late."

I gather up my things and wave to Tripp as I get into

my car.

~*~

I walk towards the entrance of the building and notice Nickolai sitting on one of the benches outside. He is carrying two cups of Starbucks coffee. I wonder who the other one is for. He looks up and sees me. His smile brightens up his face, and the fluttery feeling in my stomach starts back up again.

As I reach where he is sitting, he stands and holds out a cup of coffee to me.

"Caramel Macchiato?" He smiles.

"How did you know this is my favorite?" I'm not about to tell him I just finished having one.

"I asked Tripp yesterday." He nods his head in the direction of the parking lot.

Tripp walks toward us. His knowing grin is plastered on his face.

"So, I forgot something last night." Nickolai says bringing my attention back to him.

"What?"

"Would you like to go out again tonight? His smile is becoming infectious. I smile up at him.

"I would love to." I blush slightly.

I take his hand and walk into the building with him, ready to start the work day with a huge smile on my face.

CHAPTER 6

Nickolai

Being able to get this assignment is bitter sweet. I get to be near my family again, but I know what I am about to do will change the lives of many people in this building. This is only going to be the second time this has ever been achieved. The first went off without a hitch and no one was the wiser. This time it was my turn to assist in the organization of a new mass Awakening.

The plan is simple since I found out that what needs to be done. It will be undetectable by taste or smell. The company has hired a mobile coffee company to come in to serve coffee and other beverages. The perfect opportunity to get a mass of people all at once. The tricky part is the assistance that would be needed afterwards, but I have an idea.

My desk is cluttered with various manila envelopes, mostly employee files. I almost knock over my coffee cup as I pull a manila folder out of the stack. The items up on my computer were mostly of the task at hand, but did not have anything to do with the work the company thought I was doing.

I picked up my cell and dialed the number listed for support.

"Yes?"

"Hey Brian, this is what I am thinking we need to do for this to work.

"I'm listening."

"First, those that were already scouted by the seeker as having some Fae or Were, need to be separated from the rest. They should have a green voucher," I tell him.

"Ok, but what about those that are here as your support?" Brian asks.

"Those will be blue vouchers, just like those that do not fit the criteria."

"Ok what about the others?"

"The others will have pink vouchers."

"Ok I will get these printed out and distributed tonight. I have the list from the seeker with me. I will make sure they are distributed properly," Brian says.

"Good deal. I'll talk to you soon," I reply.

I called the next number on my list.

"Hey Drew. Great acting yesterday."

"Cha. You know it bro," Drew quips.

"Have you gotten everything squared away with Sarah at the coffee company?"

"Oh yeah, she is a smart one, wasn't she Awakened a few months ago?"

"Something like that. I need you to give her the color codes for distribution," I inform Drew.

"Ok give it to me, I'll pass it on."

"One drop from each vial for the pink. One drop from the blue vial for the green. Nothing for the blue."

"Got it boss man. Everything else set up?"

"I have one last call to make and all should be ready, I hope."

This last call would set everything in motion. I already have reservations about doing this the way Morcant wants. It almost feels like a violation. These people will not get the choice the rest of us were given, it will be forced. Quite the rude awakening, literally.

Avalon is the one I truly worry about. I don't know who is on the Fae list. The other list is just of young people. She will be on the list but I'm not sure which one. I really don't want her involved in this. I will just switch whatever she gets with mine so she won't be affected.

Just as I am about to make my last call, Melanie sits on the edge of my desk, her skirt rising up a little too high. I clench my fist under my desk. The smell of a lustful woman is intoxicating and hard to resist, but I manage to quiet the beast within.

"Nickolai, would you like to have lunch with me? I know your new and don't know many people. I just want you to know that I would love to get to know you better." She rubs her hand over my left forearm lightly.

"I am going to be really busy today, maybe a rain check?"

I don't want to be rude to her and I'm not sure how to let her down gently. I don't ever plan on cashing that rain check but she doesn't need to know that.

Melanie's face falls and then brightens back up. "I'll take you up on that rain check. Maybe after you have finished the project you have been working on so hard, you'll be up for it." She smiles at me and saunters off.

How much had she overheard? In full panic mode, I assess the situation. I don't remember smelling anyone approach me when I was on the phone, but I was preoccupied. Another thought crosses my mind. No one knows who Morcant' seeker is. The one that can detect anyone that has even an inkling of Fae or Were heritage. It might be Melanie for all I know. Maybe that is why she gets under my skin and annoys the hell out of me. It is like I have my own personal stalker. This would explain why she is always popping up where ever I go, possibly keeping tabs on me for Morcant. I need to be more careful.

I make sure no one else is nearby and dial the number to cleanup.

"Chris, its Nickolai."

"Hello Nickolai. When is the next phase scheduled?" Chris asks.

"The next phase is scheduled tomorrow. I will need your crew in at 9:30 tomorrow morning to start gathering up those that show signs."

"One moment, I have someone at my desk."

I am abruptly put on hold.

"Ok continue." Chris states as he comes back on the line.

"Well, we need to have them quarantined to move as soon as they are reoriented. I would like to have them all moved out before 3pm. Make sure we have several windowless vans," I state firmly.

"I know how to do my job, just make sure yours is done correctly and efficiently," Chris replies sharply.

The other end of the line cuts off abruptly as the receiver is slammed down.

I sigh in frustration. I'm glad this will all be over soon. Then I can get away and focus on my new relationship with Avalon. My mind drifts off as I start to think of all the possibilities of life free of Morcant and his people.

CHAPTER 7

Avalon

I feel just as nervous tonight as I did last night. I go through my entire closet and finally settle on a black print, semi-transparent, shirt with a black satin tank top, dark blue jeans and black boots. One might think my favorite color is black with what I wear but it's not. My favorite color is the same as the ocean in the Caribbean, the clear bluish-green water that I've seen in photos. It makes me want to go there.

I pay closer attention to my make-up tonight than I usually do. I have no blemishes to cover, but I want to accentuate my eyes more. I pick out mauve and green tones to blend together and the result makes my dark hazel eyes seem bright, they appear to be lighter around the pupil than normal. With my hair straight and pinned back on the sides to keep my hair out of my face, I assess my appearance. Much better than normal. I smile.

I grab my keys and head to the car. I feel nervous

letting anyone but family know where I live. Some might say it is my way to control my situation. I think I just have trust issues. I hope Nickolai is as understanding as he seems. I feel kind of bad for requesting to meet him again for our date instead of letting him pick me up. I don't feel ready for that just yet.

I pull up to the parking lot in front of Café Athens, but I do not see him waiting near the door. I don't see him anywhere. I check the clock, I'm a few minutes early. I step out of the car. I can smell his cologne, Drakkar, it makes me want to turn into a puddle right there on the spot.

"Hey beautiful."

I blush. I don't see myself as beautiful, just everyday me. I stay quiet for a moment not really knowing what to say.

"Hi!" I smile up at him. God, that sounds so stupid, but I'm not sure what else to say. Thank you, just didn't seem right.

We walk together into the restaurant. All the booths are full but the tables in the middle of the restaurant are open. We sit down at one of the tables near the bar and look over the menu.

"What is good here?" Nickolai looks at me.

"I am not sure. This is my first time here too, but I have always wanted to try it. I used to love going to the Greek festival out in Stockton when it came around every year. My suggestion would be to try the Souvlaki gyro, if you don't like lamb, then try the beef gyro."

"Hmm sounds interesting. Where is Stockton?"

"It's a city to the east of San Francisco about an hour to an hour and a half depending upon who is driving." I giggle.

"Lead foot?"

I laugh. "Sometimes, it usually happens when I am by myself in the car and a good song comes on."

The waitress comes to take our order and we both order the Souvlaki. Just as the waitress leaves the sound of a chair scraping the floor at the next table fills our ears. I look over and sigh in frustration.

"Hi you two!"

"Hi Melanie," I mutter.

I try not to let her presence bother me like usual. Why couldn't she just go away? The last two times I could chalk up to coincidence. This time is a bit much. I try to temper the bubbling anger inside me that is just wanting to explode.

"Sup." Nickolai responds with a nod of his head.

The fact that he barely acknowledges her brings my spirits back up. The hurt and angry look that just passed on her face almost makes me want to burst into a fit of giggles. Our food arrives and we dig in. With the light chatter of the restaurant and what appears to be a gnawing hunger in Nickolai's stomach there is no need for talking.

After dinner we walk the promenade to enjoy the night air and each other's company before our movie starts. We like the same movie genres, books, art, video games, sports, I could go on. No wonder spending time with him seems to get easier every day. It almost feels like I am spending time with the other half of myself.

We walk inside the theater and purchase tickets for Riddick. At the concession counter we order a large cherry coke to share and head on into the theater. Both of us want to actually see the movie, so we sit towards the front but in the center of the theater, far away from any couples in the back that would be a distraction. We are there early and the preview quizzes are up on the screen. We answer them, competing with each other. It feels good to be able to open up with someone other than Tripp. I haven't been able to do this in a long time.

The theater starts to darken with the start of the theatrical previews. The smell of buttered popcorn is everywhere. There is a sound of a group of people shuffling our way. I look past Nickolai and Melanie and her clones are headed this way.

"Melanie, I think we should sit away from them, they are on a date!" I hear Brittany hiss at Melanie. The look on Britany's face made it clear to me she didn't want to do this.

Melanie continues to come our way, obviously ignoring the not so quiet hiss from Britany, and sits down on the other side of Nickolai. She smiles a greeting at us and waves at me. Her friendliness and not so covert way of inserting herself in my date is striking my last nerve. I wait to see if Nickolai will get up to move and sit on the other side of me, to make a point to Melanie, but he doesn't. Nickolai turns toward the girls and says a few polite words and then sits back to watch the previews.

I'm so preoccupied with Melanie nearby and my anger, that I am not even watching the movie much. I'm too busy looking at her and Nickolai to enjoy the movie. A suspenseful moment occurs in the movie and I watch Melanie almost jump into Nickolai's lap. Although he shifts away from her, the action makes me livid. I've had enough of Melanie and she will find out just how much after the movie.

I stand up just as the movie ends. Nickolai looks at me because he knows I like watching past the credits to see if there is anything afterwards. I think the look on my face says it all. He gets up and grabs his jacket and walks out with me. We walk outside and it looks like he is about to say something when Melanie and her clones walk up.

"That was a great movie wasn't it?" Melanie looks at me with a glint in her eye. She is sipping on her pop from the theater.

"Actually it wasn't, because you keep inserting yourself on our dates. Haven't you gotten the clue yet that Nickolai isn't interested in you? Or are you really that stupid?"

"I don't know what you are talking about." Melanie blinks at me innocently.

"You know perfectly well what I'm talking about. You seem to be enjoying your pop." I eye her up and down. "I hope you choke on it." I glare at her. All I want to do is kick the shit out of her so she would leave us alone. I don't because I would probably land myself in jail for assault.

Melanie starts coughing, then pop starts pouring out of her mouth and nose. Her face starts to turn blue. Shit! I didn't think this would happen, I don't want her dead! I look at Nickolai and he is glancing from me to Melanie, his face bearing the look of panic. Melanie isn't just choking on pop, she is drowning in it.

"I'm so sorry, I didn't mean for this to happen!" I start panicking. At that moment, Melanie starts coughing and the pop stops pouring out everywhere.

Melanie looks at me incredulously. "What the hell are you talking about? I sucked pop down the wrong pipe. Don't flatter yourself." She pushes me away as if I have a disease.

Nickolai takes me by the arm. "We'd better go, its better if you went home after this. We can talk about what happened tomorrow if you want.

I nod and walk numbly to the car.

"I'll see you tomorrow morning." Nickolai kisses my forehead and helps me into the car before walking away.

He must think I'm a freak. Hell, with what is going on lately, I beginning to think I'm a total freak. I give myself a few minutes to get myself together before I start my car and head home.

CHAPTER 8

Nickolai

I watch from my car as she sits there trying to get herself together. So many questions are running through my mind. I don't want this girl to be involved, at least not with Morcant and his people. Is it possible that she is already Awakened?

I know I need to make sure her voucher is blue tomorrow. If she has been Awakened, I would hate to see what another dose would do to her. If her voucher is blue, it would make me wonder how the seeker missed her. Then it hits me. Maybe she is the seeker. I swear. Not knowing who the seeker is driving me crazy!

I follow her home to make sure she is ok. Seeker or no, I can't help the feelings that I have for this girl. After she gets out and goes to her apartment, I drive through the lot and head on out to the mountains. I don't know when I will be able to get my next run in with what will happen tomorrow but the beast within wants to hunt.

I park my car in the parking lot for Dowdy Lake and hike out on foot. It is dark and quiet out. It seems as if the animals nearby can sense what I am. I pass the residential area near Crystal Lake and take off into the woods. I reach a dense patch of trees and can't see any homes. I start to strip down. I'm losing control, the beast wants out now. I know I don't have enough control and focus to shift with my clothes on.

I place my clothes in a pile next to a nearby tree and the area around me starts to shift into various shades of grey. The pain lasts but a moment before the ground is much closer to my face. I feel like more of a spectator at this point and I am glad there is no one around to confront the beast. The last bit of my control wavers and the beast takes over, I'm no longer participating, I get to watch and wait until he is done.

I catch the smell of deer downwind and I feel my body launching forward and running at a break neck pace. The slight breeze in the air is filled with the animal's scent. The tall grasses will help conceal me once I get closer, though I am not sure how the green grass will mask my orange and black striped body. I come to a small pond and there it is. A young stag, whose rack is not quite filled in yet. It is doubtful he really knows how to use it yet.

I creep quietly through the tall grass, keeping my eyes on the prize. The wind shifts suddenly and the stag's head bolts upright. I've lost the element of surprise. I lunge forward and grasp the stag's hind quarters with my front paws. The tearing sensation of flesh beneath my claws feels wonderful. The anticipation of its flesh soon filling my mouth grows stronger.

My strong powerful jaws finally find purchase in the deer's throat. I feel the deer's death throws as it tries to pitch underneath my body. With its throat torn open, I know it will not be long before it lies still. The thrill of the hunt is what keeps my attention, what happens afterwards I give over to the beast and allow instinct to take control.

I wake up. It looks like it is about three in the morning. The vile taste in my mouth from the raw meat of the beast's kill makes me retch. I enjoy the thrill of the hunt, but this aftermath I've never enjoyed. I stop retching and look over, finding my pile of clothes next to me. I check my body and I seem perfectly fine except that I'm dirty and naked. I quickly put on my jeans and undershirt and run back to the car. Today is going to be a long day and I still have plenty to do before work starts.

CHAPTER 9

Avalon

I feel warm as I am being held. I scoot in closer loving the warmth and protectiveness that the arms around me make me feel. The smell of the one holding me is different than anything I can remember smelling before. It is a pleasant smell, sort of like sandalwood and musk, with a hint of something else I'm unable to identify. My heart rate increases as I realize that this is not a dream. Someone is in my apartment! I start to panic and the comfort of the arms vanish.

My eyes pop open but there is no one here on the bed with me. I sit up and look around, there is no one in the room but me. I glance over and notice there is an indentation of another body next to mine on the bed. My anxiety increases and my pulse quickens with the proof that there is, or was someone in my apartment. I get up quickly grabbing the baseball bat out of my closet and go search my small apartment. I scan the living room and kitchen, nothing is out of place. There is no evidence that anyone was in there. I move to the bathroom and look inside. There is no one here.

My pulse starts to slow down as I sink to the floor ready to scream with the scare I just had. All I can do is cry. I'm not just crying about this scare, it was just the icing on the proverbial cake. It's all the weird things that has been happening to me and around me lately that make me feel like this. If anything else goes wrong I think will need to go into a facility for the mentally disabled!

I pull myself together, wipe my face and start to get ready for work. By the time I feel presentable, I have twenty-five minutes left before I need to be at work. Thank God, I only live ten minutes away. I grab my purse and my car keys and head out the door. I only wish I had time to grab a coffee before I really start my day.

I walk up to my car but before I can put my key in the lock a sleek black mustang pulls through the parking lot and stops behind my car. Buddy, I do not have time for this today. Move your car out of my way before I really want to put a dent in it. The window rolls down and the perturbed look I know I had on my face vanishes. It's Nickolai.

"Want a ride?" Nickolai asks with a smile on his face.

I don't even need to take a second to think about it. The smile on his beautiful face is so welcoming after the start I had earlier.

"Sure!" I walk over to his vehicle and he pops open the door for me. I had thought he would think me the total freak that I am after what happened last night. Guess he's not bothered by the freak that is me.

I sit down in the car and close the door.

"Seat belt." He says quickly.

"Do you plan on gunning it out of here or something?" I look at him warily.

"No, just put your seatbelt on. I feel better knowing you're as safe as possible."

I smile at him and put my seatbelt on. "Ok, ready."

Nickolai grins back at me and starts his car forward.

"Look, about last night, I know you probably think I am a freak, but I am glad we can still be friends after that."

Nickolai stops the car abruptly, my head hits the back of the seat.

"What are you talking about? Of course we are friends, but I was hoping we were more than that." He looks at me.

The look he gives me is intense. It makes me nervous and giddy all at the same time.

"Well after the weirdness and all, I wasn't sure you would want to be more than that." I look back at him, hoping he will think I'm being silly.

"It was a freak accident, and yes it was a little weird that pop was pouring out of her like that. You didn't have anything to do with that." He looked at me seriously, like he wanted me to drop the direction I was heading in with my train of thought.

"Hell, even I was hoping she would choke on her pop. She was getting on my last nerve last night, but I was trying to be nice. I was, however, wondering when she would reach your breaking point to be honest." Nickolai chuckles a little

I sigh in relief.

"Feel better? You can stop blaming yourself now. We are just fine." Nickolai leans over and kisses me. The softness of his lips caress over mine. I lightly bring his lower lip into my mouth with a slight suction and then nibble on it.

"Don't tease, we have to go to work." Nickolai laughs and I grin up at him. Nickolai takes my hand in his and gives it a squeeze before he starts the car forward again.

"I have some things to do tonight but would you like to go out tomorrow night?"

"Sounds good to me. I want to spend some time with my dad tonight anyway."

"It's a date then." Nickolai smiles and I feel all warm inside.

CHAPTER 10

Melanie

There is an unusual buzz around the office. It must be the excitement of the free coffee, which is as good as Starbucks, and the pastries that generally went along with it. Coffee, I could do. Pastries, however, is not on the menu. There is no way that I'm going to put those sweet but fattening things in my body. I'm proud of the fact that I keep my body up like a well-oiled machine. The strict regimen that I keep myself under shows.

The aroma of espresso fills the air as people get their drinks in the break room. I watch and wait, and follow Avalon as she leaves our team to go get her coffee. I feel I have one more shot to get her to blow up at me only this time in front of everyone at work. If I can get her to do that, then maybe it will be enough to damage her reputation at work and then Nickolai will think twice about wanting to be involved with her. Especially if he wants to continue to move up in the company.

I reach the break room and see that all the supervisors are already here like they normally are when we have these type of events. They are all sipping on coffee, eating pastries and gabbing away. Did they not have any work to do? Nickolai is the only one not doing the normal supervisor thing. He is shifting his weight on the balls of his feet near the baristas and holding a blue voucher. Is he nervous about something? Maybe he is making sure everyone is served timely and sent back to their desks to continue working.

I look behind me and spot Avalon walking in alone. Where is Tripp? Oh yes, grandma's funeral. No buffer for Avalon. Making her look bad is going to be a cake walk now. I grin.

Avalon stands behind me and carries a green voucher. I wonder what all the different colors are for as I examine my pink one. I walk up to the counter as one of the baristas calls for the next person.

Nickolai approaches one of the baristas and hands her his voucher and whispers something to her. The barista calls up the next person in line. I find it odd that he gave his blue voucher to the barista but didn't have a coffee in his hand. Avalon walks up and orders her coffee. I order a chai and hand my voucher to the barista. I walk over and stand next to Avalon to wait for my drink to be done.

"Avalon? Caramel Macchiato."

"Melanie? Chai."

The two of us go up to get our drinks. Avalon takes hers first and drops off her green voucher. The barista takes the voucher and puts it on the top of the stack where mine was placed. I pick up my drink and notice that Avalon stops for a moment to take a sip of her coffee. It is the perfect opportunity to strike. I bump into her hard, and she spills her coffee down the front of her cream colored sweater. She screams from the hot liquid and instantly pulls the sweater away from her body. All eyes stare in our direction.

"Oh no, I'm so sorry! I'll pay for another coffee and a new sweater." I offer.

After what happened last night, I know she can see right through my false sincerity.

"Don't worry about it. It's not like you did it on purpose." Avalon's tone drips with sarcasm.

I can see the tears starting to surface on her eyes.

A barista hands her another coffee, this time with a lid. "We all have clumsy moments." The barista smiles at Avalon. "Don't' worry it's on the house." The barista went back behind the counter and puts all the vouchers on the table into a pouch.

Well, that did not work out quite as I had hoped. My plans dashed, I watch Nickolai as he watches Avalon leave. I see him glance at her chest, her coffee in her hand, and the empty cup on the floor. He looks at me and notices I still have my full cup in my hand. A funny look passes across his face before it changes and he frowns at me as he approaches where I am standing.

"I said I was sorry. Like I can't have a clumsy moment? I even offered to buy her a new sweater and a coffee, but the barista gave her a new one."

"What did you say?"

"Are you surprised that I was being nice?"

"That isn't what I meant. That was actually very nice of you. You said she got another coffee?"

"Yeah, the barista said it was on the house, but I saw her slip Avalon's green voucher in the pouch. I had assumed you bought her first one with your blue voucher since you weren't given a coffee. So it really wasn't on the house was it?"

A look of panic crosses his face briefly. He quickly leaves following after Avalon. Well that was a bit strange. I shrug and sip my chai. I glance around the room, there is no one worth talking to here. I walk back to my cubicle and return to work.

I start to feel sick. I check the clock to see if I have waited too long to eat again. I notice it has only been an hour since I went to get coffee and two hours since breakfast.

I reach for the apple on my desk. I am about to bite into it when I get a big whiff of something that smells completely rotten. I inspect the apple in my hand but it looks fine. I take a plastic knife out of my desk drawer and cut into it. The apple looks fine but the rotten smell increases. I look around for the source of the smell but I do not see anything that should be letting off such a foul smell. I pick up a slice of apple, bring it to my mouth, and that is when the foul stench grows worse. It has to be the apple!

I get up and go to the bathroom to throw the apple away. The farther away from my desk, the better. I get to the bathroom and the lights and sounds in the building start to affect me. It's like I have a really bad migraine. Just as swiftly the urge to retch comes to me. I run into the nearest stall. I try to retch but just keep dry heaving. The pain is becoming unbearable. I need to get to a darker, quieter place.

The supply room near the bathroom is the closest place I can think of that would be quiet. I can turn out the lights in there and keep people out of it. I take off to the supply room and open the door. I start to walk into the supply room and I notice Avalon go into one of the small conference rooms at the end of the hall. Maybe she is having the same reaction I am. I can't fault the girl for wanting to hide.

I close the door, turn off the automatic light and drop to the cold hard floor. I lean up against the door. I just need to sleep, sleep always makes the migraine go away. Instead of sleeping, I start to feel uncomfortably hot. The heat intensifies, like I'm in a sauna that is cranked up too high.

I start shedding my layers of clothing off. It doesn't help with the heat. I feel as though I'm growing exponentially hotter by the second. My whole body feels like it is now on fire. I'm down to my bra and underwear but I refuse to go further than that. Especially when I can't lock the door.

I hear screaming, growling and running noises outside the door. There is a scraping sound on the other side of the wall, as if someone is scraping something hard against it as they walk by. The increasing pain is enough that I can't care what is happening to anyone else right now.

I lay down on the cold cement floor, the brief coolness brings a momentary relief before the heat begins to grow again. I feel my skin because it feels like my flesh is crisping off. It isn't. It feels like I'm cooking from the inside out, like my blood is boiling. The pain is unbearable. I cry through the pain. I try to wipe my eyes and realize I can't move. Sheer panic takes over. This is not how I wanted to die! I'll be found in my underwear, charred beyond all recognition! What is happening to me? I scream as the pain becomes too much to bear.

CHAPTER 11

Nickolai

I check my watch again. The reinforcements that were supposed to arrive have not shown up. I know the effects of the "water" that was placed in the coffee will come to the surface any time now. I don't have to wonder how this will turn out with no support team in place. It will look like a massacre in here. My pulse starts to speed up as my anxiety level rises.

"Shit!" I don't care who can hear me at this point. I lock down the building with the security codes I received when I started here a few days ago. I'm not about to let what will inevitably happen in here out into the unknowing world.

I start searching the building for Avalon. I know that if she had any of the coffee that the barista gave to her, she should be feeling the effects within the next 10 minutes. I know that each Fae and Were will react differently to the "water". The effects on them will be radically different.

What isn't different and has happened in each occurrence that I have ever witnessed, is the disorientation, headaches and sickness each one experienced. This place is about to turn into a free-for-all. I need to find Avalon and fast. I round the corner of an aisle and almost run over the top of Drew in the process.

"Where is the support team?" The look of panic on Drew's face was clear.

"I don't know, they should have been here just after the coffee company arrived. It looks like it is just you and me, Brian is out today."

"Oh Shit!"

"Yeah, pretty much." I know my sarcasm doesn't help anything but it's how I feel too. "Look, can you try to find the ones that appear to have had the pink vouchers and round them up into a dark room that can be locked? Those will be the most volatile."

"Sure, but how can I tell who had pink ones?"

"Check all the rooms that have tile, cement floors or have access to cool water. The ones that have pink vouchers are going to be feeling hot very quickly, it's when they have cooled that they will be dangerous."

"Crap! You're making me round up all the new ones!" Drew motions with his fingers in quotations after saying new ones. "Those hurt!"

"They won't try to devour you. Just wolf out on them, they will back away from your stink. Usually. If not, try to stay out of their reach."

Drew sighs and runs off to check the places I mentioned for soon to be new ones.

I pass by a supply closet and I hear the screams from inside of it. The person inside sounds like Melanie but I don't have time to stop. If she is that far into her change I need to find Avalon now. I stop by her team and of course her desk is empty. I run over to the nearest conference room and check inside it. The light is off but I know someone is in there. I turn the light on and Avalon moans.

"Turn it off! This headache is the worst!"

"Do you feel sick to your stomach? Have you been dry heaving? Have you tried eating?"

"What is with the twenty questions Nickolai? I have a migraine. I don't want food. I am a little nauseous but that is normal with a migraine. Now turn off the light!" She squints up at me.

Before I can say anything more I hear a loud, ear curdling scream.

"It's time to move, now! I'll help you to where we need to go. Hell, I will carry you if I have to.

"I think I can walk, no need to be so chivalrous." She quips.

I look at her for a moment. She does not even seemed to be fazed by the noises coming from just outside this room or the screams that can be heard. I know she is going through the Awakening but this just seems different than all the others I have witnessed before. Not knowing what type of fae she will become, I know I need to get her out of here now.

I open the door of the conference room slowly to gauge our situation. The screams and noises of those that are in the process of transforming or already transformed have died down. The hallway is clear. We quickly leave the conference room and walk down the hallway. A bloody hand appears from the opening of a team of desks, it grasps the floor and pulls.

I don't recognize the old woman but the look on Avalon's face is evident that she knows her. It is clear by her age that she was provided a blue voucher. The woman sees us and starts screaming for help. As she pulls herself farther into the hallway it is evident that she will not last long. The arm she pulls herself with is the only limb she has left, the rest look like they have either been torn or chewed off. I'm surprised she hasn't already bled out. She will soon.

I walk over to the woman. "I'm so sorry." I bend down and twist her head violently, snapping her neck with an audible crack that I know Avalon can hear. Avalon shrieks, her skin takes on a greyish hue. She passes out and falls to the floor. I'm not sure if her passing out was in reaction to what I just did or what she is going through internally. I pick Avalon up and start running down the hallway. All the noise will undeniably attract unwanted attention.

I close the door of the safe room, which is at least thirty feet below the building. It is cool in here since there is no duct work down here and the room has taken on the temperature of the ground. I check Avalon for any signs of change. The color of her skin has almost gone back to normal. The only difference is that there is a faint iridescent shimmer to her skin now.

She seems to be sleeping peacefully. In the past, when someone was going through an Awakening they normally aren't able to sleep through it. By this time it is apparent what type of fae they are. I'm completely dumbfounded. Did she drink the coffee she was given or is her migraine just a coincidence?

"Water." Avalon moves slightly.

I'm not even sure how she knows there is someone in the room with her. I haven't been talking or moving around. I move to go get a bottle of water for her from the supply cabinet. I open the door to the cabinet and reach for a bottle of water. Another bottle lifts up and comes straight for me. I duck. I look around for the bottle and watch as it sails to the other side of the room where Avalon is laying.

The top of the bottle twists off and falls to the floor. The bottle, to my amazement, is still hovering in mid-air. A line of water comes out of the bottle and forms into a ball before going directly into Avalon's mouth. My jaw drops. A water fae.

This is not good. Most water fae have vampiric tendencies. I need to get a better look at her changes, because her Awakening has not been like any other I have witnessed in the past. I walk up slowly to her side and she looks up at me. Her eyes have changed. I have only seen one set of eyes that look similar to this, albeit a different color: Morcant's. Avalon's eyes are now blue and green, where the brown used to be is silver.

"Ok this is going to sound really odd, but I need to see your teeth." I look down at Avalon. I worry of what I might see next. I hope she isn't just like Morcant. Avalon looks at me like I have grown another head.

"Just do it please?"

Her eyes narrow as she continues to look at me.

"It feels like you know exactly what is going on. I've heard the screams and what sounds like large animal noises before I blacked out. After I show you my teeth which sounds really stupid, you will explain everything."

Avalon says the last bit through gritted teeth. I can feel her anger, it almost feels like it is pushing against me in waves.

Avalon shows me her teeth and I sigh in relief. No fangs. I rub my hand down my face as I prepare to tell her the truth and my entire involvement. I start with what I know, that is always best when you want someone to trust you.

"To be honest, I'm not sure where to start, so I will start from where I became involved in all this. I just hope you won't hate me after I tell you everything." I look at her and she motions impatiently for me to continue.

"I was in the military at the time, about two years ago. It was during shore leave when I was in San Diego. I met a man who said he could give me a better life than the military could ever offer. Of course, I was skeptical, but he kept talking about things that started to make sense to me. Different things that I could do very well, that others couldn't. Why I excelled so well at running and shooting sports. I agreed to meet with him later in the evening at a local bar called Hamilton's."

"Who was the man you were meeting at Hamilton's?"

"That is the thing. He isn't a man. He isn't human." I watched as her eyes went wide but she said nothing.

"Morcant, the person I met at Hamilton's later that night, told me of a utopian society, where others like him and myself could live free with our abilities. That we could all reach our full potentials in life without judgment. All the things he promised sounded so wonderful. I agreed to join him after my tour of duty was up. He bought me a drink to seal our deal and walked me outside. I didn't notice until after I had the entire drink that we had walked out the back and we were in a secluded area behind the bar. It was there that I was Awakened."

"What do you mean by Awakened?"

"You just went through an Awakening, albeit an odd one, but you did. Don't you notice anything different about yourself, what you can do?" I look at her.

Avalon takes a moment to take all this in. She looks at her arms and her eyes get larger.

"Ok, I remember being pale, but not this pale."

She lifts her hands up and spreads out her fingers. "Is this what I think it is?" Delicate webbing connects the base of her fingers together but it is not so noticeable that it would attract attention.

"When you get to where you have a mirror you will notice more. You also have an uncanny knack of manipulating water." I snicker, remembering the water bottle that almost hit me in the face.

"I don't understand this Awakening process, how does it work?"

"I'm not entirely sure, I don't know where the special

water comes from or why it works the way it does. If water is given to someone that has Fae or Were heritage somewhere in their family line, the water awakens that genetic code and it brings it forward. However, if the person has no Fae or Were heritage, a drop of Morcant's blood is used along with some of the water to create another race. We call them new ones. Others call them Vampires."

"Vampires!"

"Not Bram Stoker's Dracula Vampires, but yeah. All the new ones are linked to Morcant through his blood but it is a very weak link. They all follow their own code of rules. All Fae and Were use their abilities to make the collective group better."

"Were? What is that?"

"Werewolves. There are more than just wolf types of Weres."

"Wait a minute. Back up. You said you were Awakened? I don't see anything unusual about you." She raises her eyebrow up at me and cocks her head.

"Well I'm not Fae, and I'm not a Vampire. I'm Were. I am not sure how my ancestors got involved in all this but after my Awakening I wanted answers. I still do."

Avalon looks at me in disbelief. "Prove it." She challenges.

CHAPTER 12

Avalon

Everything Nickolai is saying seems to be all too surreal. The fact that he was Awakened two years ago yet shows no outward sign of being different is a bit hard to believe. So of course, I dare him to prove it. I know he is not finished telling all he needs to tell but I have to see it to believe it.

"Just remember, what your about to see is still me, and I will never hurt you." Nickolai tells me.

I nod my head even though I'm not sure what to expect next. Nickolai's form starts to move and transform. Orange, black and white fur starts to sprout out of his skin. There is a cracking noise as his bones contort and reform to its new shape. I cringe, it sounds so painful. I open my eyes back up and scramble backwards placing myself tight up against the wall.

"A Tiger!" I scream out. It takes me a moment to

process what Nickolai had said before. I move slowly away from the wall. I notice the eyes in the beast are the same as Nickolai's except for that there is a golden glow around the pupil. I tentatively reach out and wait to see if the tiger moves. It doesn't. I move further and put my hand on the tiger's neck.

The tiger starts purring and I release the breath that I didn't realize I was holding. The tiger then rubs its head up against my body. It relieves some anxiety I have but I am still not happy with him. From what I've heard it feels like he knows a whole lot more of this crazy situation than I do.

"Ok you've proved it, now change back so you can finish telling me everything."

I push the tiger away and sit back down on the pallet on the side of the room. Nickolai regains his human form and sits down across from me.

"How is it you can transform into something like that and not lose your clothes?"

"Not everything works like what happens in the Twilight movies."

I snicker. I visualize Nickolai's clothes bursting off and my thoughts trail off. It starts to get warm in the room, or maybe it's just me. Hah!

"I have to focus and concentrate that way every time I shift and then shift back my clothes that I was wearing before the shift are still on me. Of course when I was first Awakened that isn't the way it happened. It actually was close to the Twilight movies you girls like to watch. I learned later that I could keep them on and not destroy all the clothes I own." Nickolai grins.

Did he know the direction that my thoughts just went? Does he have other supernatural abilities? I shake myself out of my thoughts, there is more to this that I have to know.

"Ok so continue." I look at him seriously. I'm having a hard time being mad at him.

"First off, I didn't want you involved in this. I tried very hard to keep you out of it. The first day we met, how the coffee didn't spill and the incident with Melanie after the movie, I was almost sure you had some Fae heritage. I just did not know what kind. The control you exhibited made me think you were already Awakened like me, or that you were someone else entirely."

"Who did you think I was?"

"Well there is a person we call the seeker. This seeker, no one knows who he or she is. We just know the seeker exists. The seeker can tell upon meeting a person if they are unique. Whether that is being Fae or Were it doesn't matter. Once they are identified they are put on a list to recruit. Sometimes, Morcant will do the recruiting himself. Our group believes the seeker is Morcant's right hand. It's like wondering if you are walking around with a spy watching you all the time."

"Why are you worried about a spy if you are on the same side?"

"That is the thing. I don't think I am on the right side anymore. A year ago a plan was played out and mass recruitment of Vampire, Fae and Were was completed within a night. All of us thought it was so awesome that we grew so quickly. I jumped at the chance to do the same thing here."

I stiffen at the thought of that many Vampires and

other deadly beings all in one place. It registers what he just said, that he did the same thing here.

"Do what exactly?" My eyes narrow at him. I'm not sure I like where this is going.

"Well, after I volunteered to help coordinate this recruitment, I was told exactly how people were recruited so quickly. Avalon, those people weren't recruited! They were forced to change, they were not given the choice to accept it like I was."

"The Awakening?"

"Yes, once you're Awakened nothing is ever the same again. Your new found abilities get in the way of that. When I found out, I wanted to go back to what I was before, but I couldn't. I knew I would be branded a traitor and probably killed for my actions."

"Why would they kill you for refusing to force people into changing? Except for the forcing part it doesn't sound all that bad."

"I haven't told you everything yet. When vampires feed on humans until they die, they are punished for it, they receive the final death."

"What is the final death?"

"Final death is what a Vampire can't come back from. Yes, you can snap their neck and that would kill most people, it does not kill them, they regenerate and come back."

"Oh," I say.

"Our rules are strict and we are expected to obey.

There is another reason for this mass recruitment. Two centuries ago, Morcant found that if he fed on Fae that it would extend his life and keep him young but only for about fifteen years, then he would start to age. A century ago, he happened upon a recruit that turned out to have Fae heritage from both parents, of different varieties. He found that feeding from this type of Fae it would sustain him much longer, and he is looking for another to feed on so that he doesn't start aging."

"So all of this is just so that he can stay young?"

"It is only some of the story. The way he is amassing people looks more like he is trying to build an army. I'm not sure why though. I don't plan on fighting in a war that I know nothing about. I'm not sure if he already suspects that I am wavering in my loyalty. However, it would explain why the promised support teams did not show up today."

"Support teams? What do they support?"

"The support teams are teams of specialized Fae, Were and Vampire that contain and teach the new recruits how to behave within our society. They also keep them contained through their Awakenings and away from the public. That is why there is a virtual zoo up there." He points to the ceiling. "It's why there will be so many deaths and it's all my fault." He looks at me pleadingly.

His entire posture looks like one of defeat. It's so different from how I normally see him; strong and confident.

"I don't think it's entirely your fault. What choice would you have had except death if you didn't do it?"

"None." Nickolai mutters. "It still doesn't keep this from making me look so selfish that I would ruin and risk so many lives just to save mine."

I don't have time for what seems to be the start of his pity party. Yes, I'm angry at him for agreeing to do this to so many people. I can't hate him for it though. How would I have dealt with this if I had been put in his position? I'd like to think I'd be selfless and put others before me. I really don't know that I would though.

"So how did you try to keep me out of this?" I try to alter the direction of the conversation just a little bit.

"When I tried to convince you that the incident with Melanie was just some freak choking accident. I also ordered your coffee for you today with my voucher. The coffee I ordered with my voucher would not have caused an Awakening in you, because nothing would have been added to it. I saw that you had a green voucher which meant Fae, so I tried to switch it. When Melanie made you spill your coffee, you were given a new one. Unfortunately the barista that gave it to you used your green voucher."

"Well I do not blame you for all of this. Thank you for trying to keep me from it." I want to hold him and bring him comfort but my anger is not going to allow it.

Nickolai starts to look relieved and walks over to me. I hold out my arm stopping him from coming closer.

"However, I'm not happy that you have been lying to me this whole time. Yes, I know it's only been a few days but still! It makes me wonder what else you're hiding from me." I cross my arms over my chest.

"That is it I swear! Now you know more than my family does, they don't know about any of this. They just think

I got lucky and landed a job close to home." Nickolai sighs and puts his head in his hands.

"So with all your vast knowledge, what am I now?" I spit out sarcastically.

"It is hard to say, you didn't experience the Awakening as violently as others I have seen. Yours was mild in comparison. The water ability, no fangs, and the slight webbing in your fingers and I suspect your toes, would indicate Merrow heritage."

"What the hell is a Merrow and why would I have fangs?"

"Some water Fae have fangs and are almost like Vampires. They drink human blood to sustain their youth. Merrows are a different type of water Fae and there different types of Merrows. Since you did not sprout fur you aren't a Selkie, so that would make you a Mermaid."

I bust out laughing at that. "A Mermaid? You can't be serious. Do I look like I have a tail to you?"

"Out of water, mermaids don't have tails. I wonder why you didn't seek more water. I can't tell if you have scales because you are wearing jeans. I guess you will find that out later. What's weird is most mermaids have green skin and hair, yours is the same color as it has been there is just a silvery shimmer to it now."

"I know you have a theory as to why I don't look the way I should. I can see the gears churning in your head."

"The reason I think you don't look completely like a Mermaid is because you are more than one type of Fae, and it scares the shit out of me. I think they are taking equal control so your appearance isn't changing."

My eyes widen in alarm. Food for the master, just great!

"I'm not going to turn you over to him Avalon, so get the thought out of your head. Not turning you in however, will label me as a traitor. Is there someplace we can go after we leave this place that no one knows about? Once I leave and disappear, it will be known I have defected and they will be hunting me down."

"Well we can always go to my dad's, no one has been there, not even Tripp."

"Sounds like a plan, let's get your things and go. With all that has happened, things should be dying down up there. The only ones that will be still roaming around won't like the smell of you or me for dinner."

I quickly grab my things, thankful I brought my small purse with me to the conference room when I had the headache. I wonder what ones he is referring to.

"Ready?"

I nod. I'm not really ready, but I can't stay in this room forever.

Nickolai goes to the door and listens for a moment before opening it. He pauses for a moment and sniffs the air. I snicker. He glares at me to be quiet. He smiles slightly as if he just realizes what it is that I find funny. Nickolai points in the direction we need to go and walks out of the room.

What little I can see before me doesn't look like I'm still at work. The walls are made of earth as well as the ceiling. It looks like the place is wired for basic electricity but it doesn't seem to be working. The air is cool like the mining tunnels in Georgetown that I visited with my dad in July. A shiver goes down my spine. The coolness and the tunnel also reminds me of the nightmares I've been having recently.

Nickolai leads me down the tunnel. His vision must be enhanced by his abilities since he is able to navigate through here so easily. After many twists and turns he finally stops and holds me still. He cocks his head to one side as he is listening intently for something. He puts his hand out and pushes on the wall. It moves!

Light pours in and I recognize the hallway. It's the first floor of my building. This is where the head honcho of CommTech has his corner office that has large windows that give him an excellent view of the Rocky Mountains. Nickolai covers the opening with the large landscape picture of the mountains. No one would ever know of the secret place behind the picture unless they were shown it. I wonder what other secrets are in this building.

A slight whine, like a hurt dog comes from my right, brings me out of my thoughts. No time to search out more secrets. I turn to look to see what is making the whining sound. My eyes widen at what I see. A large timber wolf is laying down next to the cubicle wall that makes up part of the hallway. The wolf's legs on his right side look bent at odd angles.

"Drew! Man, what happened? Nickolai rushes to the wolf's side.

"Drew?" I looked at Nickolai incredulously. "He is involved in this too?"

"Drew has been one of my good friends since high school but didn't want to go into the service when I did." Nickolai starts explaining.

"When did he get Awakened?" I cut in.

"You know this really isn't the time or place to be talking about this right now. We need to be getting out of here." Drew grimaces in pain, back in his human form.

I blush slightly at the admonition. Thankful that Drew was able to focus enough to keep his clothes on, I walk over to Nickolai and assist him in helping Drew up. It is definitely lopsided support with my being so short but he'll have to make do. We hobble down the hallway and come across a small, hair and skin mass in the floor.

"What the hell is that?" I point to the thing in the floor and look at Nickolai.

"Not what, who." Nickolai sighs. "From the looks of it this person was in transition."

"Transition into what? I've never seen anything like that before." Drew looks at Nickolai.

Nickolai inspects the body closer along with the blood stained the floor. Bits of the body is ripped off and laying haphazardly around it. Nickolai scrunches up his nose for a moment.

"A Leprechaun, see his limbs are shortened but his head didn't complete the change before he was attacked.

"I don't remember anyone in the office with red hair and thick side burns." Drew says.

"Before the changes, he didn't have them. His transformation wasn't complete." Nickolai shakes his head sadly.

"Who is he? You must know since you know how to tell what he was turning into." Drew looked at Nickolai.

"Neville Brown."

My eyes widen in shock. He was my supervisor!

"What did this to him?" I ask.

"A new Were, hard to say if it was wolf, cat or something else. When a person first takes on were form, they generally lose control and run on instinct. When there is no one to control them, this happens." Nickolai states matter-of-factly.

It almost sounds like Nickolai can just flip a switch and not be bothered by what he is seeing. Right now I wish I could do that. I wish I could've not seen this.

CHAPTER 13

Melanie

I wake up and feel the cement floor beneath me. I passed out from the pain, in a supply closet, in my underwear! I just hope no one opened that door while I was out cold. I shiver at the thought of the violation. Wait, there's no pain! I almost want to shout with glee and have a party.

A sharp pang of hunger hits me. This is a kind of hunger I've never felt before. Sure, I have done starvation diets before and was insanely hungry. This is ten times worse. With being so hot before, I'm ready to see if I left a mold of myself on the floor. That be something. I giggle. Hot enough to melt the floor. That is a new one.

I open my eyes and the room is lit with a soft blue light. I look around for the light source but find none. Weird. I get up and glance down at the floor. The soft blue light seems to be coming from above. I look up, again there is no light. The light issue is weird but at least there is no Melanie-mold in the floor. I giggle. I grab my clothes and quickly put them on. I snap the button off the top of my jeans when I try to fasten them.

"What the hell? Those are brand new!" I cry out.

I go to the door and listen for a moment. It seems quiet, no strange noises like I remember hearing before. I slowly open the door and the hallway is clear. I'm not sure what time it is because I left my cell in my purse on my desk. I look toward the windows, it is night time already!

I start to walk over towards my desk when I hear odd noises coming from all over. Some of the noises sounds like animals but they are faint, others sound like loud drumming. I look around but still did not see anything. I reach my desk as another hunger pang hits me and I feel like doubling over. I grab the banana that is on my desk, peel it and take a large bite.

"Ugh!" I spit the bite out into the trash. The banana tastes like dirt and ash in my mouth. I look at the banana and it looks perfectly fine.

Suddenly I smell something sickeningly sweet, which makes my mouth water. What is that smell? I hear someone crying nearby. I follow the smell, I don't care who is crying. I'm hungry! I come to the source of the smell and she is crying.

It's Marie! I look around her for the source of smell and find nothing. My mouth is still watering. Maria huddles under her desk hugging her legs to her chest with one arm, she is holding her neck with her other hand.

"Oh my God! You're one of them!" She cries out after looking up at me.

Her panic and movement speeds up her heartbeat. I can hear it. Blood seeps through Marie's fingers, running down her neck and arm. I feel the overwhelming urge to drink her blood. The thought sickens me for the slightest moment. Without further hesitation, I lunge forward and pin her to the floor. I yank her hand away from her throat and greedily sink my teeth into the soft warm flesh.

The warm, thick blood coats my throat. I draw in deeply taking more blood into my mouth. The taste is delicious like nothing I ever could have imagine existing before. I lose myself in satiating my hunger. Marie's body goes limp in my arms and I pull away. I look at her and her neck looks like it was mauled. I don't hear the drumming noise any longer. I bend down and put my head to her chest. Her heart isn't beating!

I back up in horror. What have I done? I feel two pricks on my lower lip. What the hell? I pick up my purse from where I dropped it earlier. I fumble inside my purse for my compact and pull it out. I flip open the compact and look at myself in the mirror. My jaw drops.

My green eyes are now glowing blue and I have fangs! I panic. I have to get out of here! I just killed Marie! I run to the hallway, ignoring the gore that is all around. I can smell it now that the hunger is gone. I run to the stair well and down the stairs, my legs can't get me out of here fast enough!

I run out of the door at the bottom of the stairwell and almost run over the top of Nickolai and Avalon supporting Drew. I look at them in panic, wondering if I am going to lose it and maul them too. A look of guilt quickly passes from Nickolai's face. Did he know what happened? I feel my anger rise and boil over.

"You know what happened today don't you!" I accuse him.

I want to throttle him. I've never been this angry before.

Nickolai loosens his hold on Drew and faces me. "Yes, but before you try to beat me into a bloody pulp, I'd like to try to make amends."

"How can you possibly make amends for this?" I gesture all around me and at myself.

I try hard not to cry.

"If you will come with us, I can help you. You will escape a life I'm sure you wouldn't want, if you stay. I'll explain things later when we are at a safer location. I promise."

His comment scares me. It seems like he has seen this before. What could be worse this this? How would my life be worse by staying?

"If you agree to come with us, you must promise never try to feed from anyone at the place we are going to. Is that understood?"

I nod my head silently, though I have no idea how I'm going to control myself. I obviously had no control when I attacked and killed Marie. I sniff and wrinkle my nose. Something here reeks! I sniff more and realize the stench is coming from them.

"If everyone smells like you guys do, I don't see that it will be a problem. No offense, you all reek!"

Nickolai tries to hold in a snort but fails miserably.

"Fine, come with us."

Nickolai takes ahold of Drew again and leads us all to a side door. Nickolai pulls out a remote and the door unlocks. I open the door and hold it open for the others. Nickolai and Avalon clumsily manage to get Drew outside. I follow them out and let the door shut. Nickolai clicks the remote again and the locking mechanism reactivates.

I think I see someone at the edge of the parking lot near the trees watching the building. I almost stumble when we move from the paved walkway to the grass. I look back up and the person is gone. I follow the group as they run as fast as Drew can hobble to Nickolai's car.

CHAPTER 14

Nickolai

The back country roads are dark with only the headlights on my car lighting our way. I have them on for other motorists and for Avalon. I don't need the headlights on. I can see perfectly fine in the dark. The night sky is sprinkled with stars and a waxing crescent moon hangs high in the sky. I turn onto Hwy 392, heading east, following Avalon's directions. The air starts to smell of cows and other animals.

"Where are we going?" Melanie scoots forward on the seat. "Could you please crack a window? She reeks of flowers and you two smell like dirty animals, it's horrible!"

"Melanie, we are going to my dad's house. It's secluded and just north of Severance. No one will know where we have gone. Rolling down the windows won't give you too much relief, it smells bad of cows outside." Avalon explains.

"I'd rather a couple of minutes smelling cow than the potent stench you all are giving off! We are almost there then?" Melanie complains.

"Yes, about fifteen more minutes." Avalon sighs.

I roll my eyes. She is still demanding. I wonder if what she did even phased her at all. The evidence is all over her, she is definitely not a neat eater. I snort at my thoughts.

"What is funny?" Avalon leans over and asks.

"I'll tell you later." I smile down at her and squeeze her hand.

I only hope we are ok after all this. I certainly wouldn't blame her if she hates me after today.

I turn the car off onto a paved road. I have no clue what road I'm on. After a few minutes, Avalon directs me to turn off onto a dirt road. I drive up the dirt road for about five minutes before I can see lights up ahead from a rather large house. Avalon tells me to pull up on the circle drive and stop in front of the house. I pull up and stop in front of the house.

I exit the car and walk around to the passenger side. I open the door to help Avalon and the others out. Avalon starts digging in her purse. I instruct Melanie to help me with Drew while Avalon goes up to the front door. I turn around helping Melanie support Drew. The large grey house looms in front of us. Most of the windows are dark but a few are lit by small lamps.

Avalon puts her key into the lock and opens the front door. She walks in and holds the door open letting us into the front room.

The room is dimly lit by a small lamp on a large oak

desk in the back left corner. I look around the room and notice
the masculine quality to the furnishings; large, bulky and bought
for comfort. The southern wall of the room is nothing but an
extremely large book case. There are works of art hung about
the room on the other walls.

Avalon quietly closes the door behind us.

A small man, about five foot seven inches, appears in
the doorway across the room. His dark brown hair is slightly
disheveled and his brown eyes focus in on us as if he is
cataloguing every detail. A look of panic crosses his face and
then is gone. I suspect the look is because of the blood that is
all over Avalon.

"Does someone want to clue me in on what is going
on? Or why you are here at three in the morning?" The man
looks to Avalon worried and tries stifling a yawn.

"Um."

"Whatever you're thinking of saying, don't. I know
when you're lying Avalon." The man crosses his arms and
looks at all of us.

"Mr. Sheehy, I am sorry to interrupt. We need to get
Drew to a stable place so that I can set his bones and he can
rest."

The man I'm assuming to be Avalon's dad looks at
Drew and uncrosses his arms. "Call me Carl. Come this way."
Carl turns around. Melanie and I follow him, carrying Drew
between us.

We walk into a hallway that runs north and south in the
house. Ahead of me there is a kitchen to the left and to the

right is a large living room. There are stairs on the far right wall of the living room, going down into what I assume is a basement. Carl turns to the right and goes up the hallway and opens up a door on the left to a room.

"He can stay in this room while he recovers. Everything he needs is accessible on this floor."

Carl looks at Drew. "The door on the south wall is your bathroom to use."

Carl eyes me curiously. "How do you know how to set bones?"

"Military experience." I don't elaborate further, and Carl seems to take my word for it.

"Very well, I'll see you in the living room in a bit." Carl exits the room but leaves the door open.

"You may want to go with him Melanie, this won't be pretty."

Melanie nods and walks out of the room.

I help Drew get comfortable on the bed.

"So how did you let this happen?" I ask him.

"I was trying to round up the new ones like you asked. There was one, however, who wasn't cooperating and so I shifted. My wolf form did not deter him either. He came at me faster than I anticipated he could. He ended up breaking my legs on my right side before he and the others with him took off." Drew says through his teeth as he hisses trying to get comfortable.

"Ouch." I look at him. "You ready for this?"

"No, but I don't really have a choice do I?" Drew snaps back.

"Not unless you want to be lame for the rest of your life. You know what will happen if you leave your bones like this and you finish healing."

Drew nods. I quickly set the bones in his lower leg and his right forearm. He howls in pain and then is silent. I look to see if he has passed out on me but he is just looking at me.

"What?"

"What are we going to do? We are going to be chalked up as deserters and they will hunt us down." The look of panic on Drew's face mirrors my own feelings.

"I'm still working on that. According to Avalon, no one knows about her father's house."

"Not even Tripp?" Drew asks.

"Not even Tripp." I say.

"You know that will not keep us hidden forever, right?" Drew says sarcastically.

"Yeah, I know. For the moment, it's all I've got." I shrug. "Get some rest, as soon as I know something or what to do, I'll fill you in."

Drew nods and then closes his eyes. I turn to walk out of the room. I get to the door and I can hear soft rumbling sounds. I snicker. Drew sure can sleep easily. I shake my head. I walk through the house and find the others in the living room.

I know I need to tell Carl what has happened. As much as I hate to admit it, I will need his help. I suspect he knows some information that will help Avalon figure out what exactly she is. With her abilities already in use before she was Awakened, he has to know something. Carl looks at me expectantly, waiting for answers.

"Do you have another guest room, preferably in a basement with little to no windows?" I ask. It still wasn't time for this talk yet. Melanie needs to be put into a safe place before morning.

Carl looks at me strangely.

"I will fill you in on everything. Right now, I need to get Melanie into a room like that soon."

"Avalon can show you the room you need. When you are done, both of you will come back up here and explain."

I nod.

CHAPTER 15

Avalon

I escort Nickolai and Melanie down to the basement, to the guest room at the north end of the house. I open the door to the small guest suite. The dark blue curtains are made of heavy material and let in very little light. It was the perfect room for when Dad had his migraines. The queen sized sleigh bed is but up against the east wall and the bathroom door is on the south wall of the room.

"This room is yours to use for however long you need it." I say quickly.

I didn't know much about the vampires like Melanie. The little information Nickolai shared earlier and the evidence that is all over her is enough to show her some kindness. Something she did not deserve, but it made me think about what I would have hoped for if our situations were reversed. If she had stayed she would have been given the final death. Though she had not said she killed anyone, the look in her eyes, the mess all over her and her posture gave it away.

"So why did I need to come down here?" Melanie looked at Nickolai with her hands on her hips.

"There is a lot that you don't know about your condition. Since we are safe here, I will tell you what I know."

"How do you know anything about what I went through?" Melanie asks incredulously.

"Because I am partly responsible for what you went through Melanie, and I'm sorry."

"What?" Melanie shrieks. "How could you?"

"It's a long story and one you really don't have time for." Nickolai says.

"What do you mean?" Melanie looks at Nickolai. The look in her eyes are pleading for answers.

"Let's go over your abilities to just confirm what you are. After that I will explain what you can expect to encounter on a day to day basis. Well, night to night anyway." Nickolai says, ignoring the look in Melanie's eyes.

"I have insane hunger that is only lessened with blood. I have fangs!" Melanie points at her elongated teeth after opening her mouth. "My green eyes are now blue. Glowing blue, I might add. I think it is pretty obvious to me what I am."

"And what do you think you are Melanie?"

"A freaking Vampire Nickolai! How is it possible that you turned me into a Vampire? I was never bitten!" Melanie looks like she is about to blow up.

"Well, you are what most people would call a Vampire. The Vampire that you are is not like Bram Stoker's Dracula." Nikolai says with a slight smile.

"Will I sparkle in the sunlight or blow up?" Melanie asks.

I laugh at this, it was just too funny. Imagining Melanie blowing up felt good. It wasn't a good thing to feel but being constantly angry with her, it felt vindicating.

Nickolai snorts out a laugh. "No, you won't sparkle. Don't be ridiculous. You girls and your Twilight novels."

Nickolai laughs more before settling down. "Sorry, that was just too much."

Melanie glares at the both of us.

"You won't blow up in the sunlight either. You will get a good sunburn but that is about it, and it will heal within minutes." Nickolai tells her.

"What else do I need to know?" Melanie looks back at Nickolai.

"Being a new Vampire, as you call it, you will need to sleep in the day time. In fact, this early on you won't have a choice, you will just become comatose as soon as the sun rises. During this time you will be weak and helpless, much like a new born babe. This problem will lessen with age. If you live long enough, you won't require sleep at all." Nickolai informs her.

"What is that supposed to mean?" Melanie puts her hands on her hips.

"It means you are not as immortal as you might think.

You can still be killed, it's just tricky." Nickolai pinches the bridge of his nose with his finger and thumb as if he is getting a headache.

"How is it tricky?" Melanie asks.

"Well for starters wood stakes do nothing. It has to be iron. The Fae have an aversion to iron. You are a mutated form of a Fae from what I have pieced together, so you also have this same aversion. The iron must pierce your heart but that is still not enough to finish you off. Your head must come off and your entire body burned."

My eyes widen in surprise. "Is that how Morcant can be killed too?" I look at Nickolai.

"I believe so, if you could get close enough to do it. I mean she was made the way she is from his blood combined with the water." Nickolai replies.

"So what your saying is, I'm tricky to kill, but I will pass out come dawn weak as a baby?" Melanie asks.

I look at her like she has multiple heads. Is that all she heard this entire time? Only about herself?

"Pretty much." Nickolai says nonchalantly.

"Ok, everyone here either reeks of animal or flowers. What about my feeding problem?" Melanie demands.

"Only new Vampires have no control over their feeding problem. Control must be learned. Blood is what you will crave the most, but all of your kind can survive on a single blood bag for a week. The rest of the time, eat raw meat that still has blood in it." Nickolai shrugs as if her food problem is no big deal.

Melanie shudders.

"What's wrong now?" Nickolai asks irritably.

"I am a vegan, I don't eat meat!" Melanie whines.

Nickolai laughs again.

"You do now. If you have tried to eat any plants yet, you will know what I am talking about. Any plants would taste like dirt or ash in your mouth. I'm not really sure, I've just heard it described that way." Nickolai shrugs.

"You still haven't told me what to do about this problem, there is no food here for me!" Melanie screeches.

"There are animals all over the place! Kill one and eat it. You'll get minor blood nourishment and raw meat. Besides, from the look of you, I'd say you had enough blood to last you over two weeks." Nickolai gestures at Melanie's body.

Melanie starts to cry.

"I didn't mean to kill her, I couldn't stop myself."

Nickolai hesitantly steps closer in attempt to console her. "You are not to blame for that. Of course you didn't want to kill her. You just do not have control over your urges yet."

"Get away from me! God! You reek Nickolai!" Melanie pushes him away.

Nickolai and I both laugh. Well I guess I don't have to worry about Melanie trying to pursue him anymore.

"Anyway, tomorrow we will start working on your

control problems." Nickolai tells her.

Melanie nods.

"For now, Avalon and I will leave you here. Dawn is almost here, might as well be comfortable on a bed instead of doing a face plant in the floor when the time comes."

I giggle and Melanie glares at both Nickolai and I.

"Come on Nickolai, quit making fun of her for something she didn't choose for herself." I grab his arm and start leading him to the door.

Instantly his face falls and I realize I just threw her condition back in his face.

CHAPTER 16

Rion

My mind won't let me rest. I can't stop thinking about what was discussed at council a few days ago. I hear the front door open and close. I know she is here with her friends. I felt her approaching several minutes ago. The others she brings with her feel strange. This strangeness was explained to me at council. Cauldron magic, a secret form of magic that was kept hidden from all but a select few. This magic was used to create Fae races such as Weres. Now it's being used to create a mutated form of water Fae, what they are calling Vampires.

Scouts reporting their detection of odd Fae power in multiple locations prompted the latest council session. These odd Fae seem to be weak versions of what they should be. The council's conclusion: that the lost treasure, the Cauldron of Dagda, is being used to create them. A cry of pain and the crack of bones being set bring me out of my thoughts.

I look around my room. The room that really isn't my

room. The beige walls are covered with drawings and wards of protection. The drawings were made of charcoal and depicted a city that can't be found in this world. On the desk and dresser were handmade wood carvings. As the voices downstairs grow quiet again, I get up from the bed and open the door.

I walk down the hall looking at the pictures of the family. Pictures that were at least four years old hung on the wall. Pictures of when the family was whole. I take the stairs one at a time, debating what I need to say to Carl.

I walk down the hallway and turn right and continue into the family room. Carl is in the kitchen fixing coffee. This early in the morning? I knew something had happened and whatever it is will not be good news.

Carl walks into the living room and hands me a cup of coffee and sets the tray down with three cups on it. He takes one of them and sits down on the couch.

"Carl, its past time to tell Avalon. She reached the age of decision in June, she should have been made aware of this sooner. I know you want to spare her but with what I can feel, we are way beyond that now." I tell him as I sit next to him on the couch.

"I have never noticed her acting strangely or anything unusual." Carl retorts.

"You haven't? I find that very hard to believe. She has displayed two abilities that I am aware of when she was just a child! She could very well be the daughter of prophesy, we can't afford to keep her in the dark any longer. The cauldron is being used to create Vampire-like Fae."

Carl gasps.

"I really doubt it is a threat to the human world right now, or there would have been instances that would have caught our attention much sooner." I try to calm him slightly.

"I don't think we could keep it from her now anyway. Once you see her, you will know what I mean." Carl mumbles.

I nod.

Voices drift up the stairs. Avalon is bringing her Were friend back up the stairs. I stand to greet them. I wait for her to notice me before I take a step forward.

Avalon notices me as she reaches the top of the stairs and runs full steam ahead and tackles me in a hug.

"Oof." I grunt as I hug her back.

I haven't seen her like this since May, when I had gone to see the Council and do some scout work. My summer school story was great cover. I go to a boarding school, my cover for my real activities.

"Oh how I've missed you!" Avalon says happily.

"Me too." I smile at her. I look over to the man that is now standing behind her with a scowl on his face. I release my hold on Avalon, even though her closeness is a great comfort.

"Are you going to introduce me to your friend?" I ask her.

"Oh, sorry. I forgot my manners. I'm just so happy to see you! Nickolai, this is my twin brother, Rion."

The scowl soon vanishes and Nickolai smiles but the smile does not reach his eyes. He walks forward and stands next to Avalon.

"Hi Nickolai, nice to meet you." I tell him.

"Hey." Nickolai nods his head in my direction.

I know I will have to watch him, he is too quiet.

I move to shake his hand when I notice the blood on their clothes and stop. "What the hell happened?" I demand in alarm.

"I think that her father has more right to ask her that, than an absentee brother." Nickolai glares at me.

I wonder if he suspects the truth.

"What I'm curious about is why Melanie is here. I thought you couldn't stand her?" Carl looks at Avalon. "Wasn't she the one you complained about making your life miserable at work?"

"Yes, but I couldn't leave her there, not like that." Avalon moves her hair behind her right ear.

"I have some questions that I need answers to, and I think you have them." Avalon looks directly at Carl.

Carl looks at me in panic. I nod in response.

"What happened? Where is there, Avalon?" I want her to open up to me.

"Let's just say that some things have happened to me fairly recently that has me questioning what I am and where we come from." She looks at me and then at Carl.

"Well my side of the family comes from Scotland. When your ancestors came to America our family settled in the Appalachian Mountains. Our family then intermingled with the Cherokee people. Your mother's family is from Ireland. When they came to America they settled in Rhode Island." Carl informs her like it he had rehearsed it.

I want to slap him, but I don't. It's like he panicked and went back to his old ways instead of coming clean. I open my mouth to speak when Nickolai's body language stops me. Nickolai growls. Can he tell that Carl is holding back the truth?

"Now that you have given the child's version of your family history, maybe you can tell her the whole truth without the veiled deception." Nickolai stands looking directly at Carl with his arms crossed over his chest.

"I don't see why you feel the need to be so rude. You have no right to speak to my dad that way." I glare at Nickolai.

"I have every right. The deception between the two of you stinks, like rotten cheese. I normally wouldn't be so disrespectful but since Avalon's life is on the line, you both need to come clean. I know you are aware of much more than you are letting on." Nickolai glares back at me.

"What do you mean her life is on the line?" I ask in alarm.

"Just what I said. My former employer is looking for people with her qualifications. Not to hire but to feed off of. He drains any Fae that have more than one Fae lineage." Nickolai says quickly.

"Oh shit!" I exclaim.

"Yeah, so you really need to come clean with what you know. This way we know what to expect and we can go from there." Nickolai glares at me and then Carl.

"Alright but to tell you, it will seem strange and may be hard to understand. I need to show you what I know. Go ahead and sit down." I motion for both of them to sit down.

Nickolai doesn't move.

"Please." I add quickly.

Nickolai follows Avalon and sits next to her.

"How are you going to show us? Did you develop abilities on our birthday and never bother to tell me?" Avalon looks at me accusingly.

I avoid her question and sit down across from them. I don't warn them of what they will experience next.

"Long ago there were a people that came to Ireland from far off islands, they seemed more advanced than those that inhabited Ireland at that time." I picture the events as they were shared with me long ago.

The room starts to darken and the air seems to be easier to breathe as the humidity increases. The walls disappear and we are surrounded by green trees, grass, and streams. Off to the north is a large rock outcropping. A light rain starts to pour and a breeze picks up carrying with it the smell of the sea.

Avalon gasps in shock. Nickolai looks uneasy. Carl looks like he is about to faint. I smile.

Off to the north near the rocks are tall, red and blonde haired people fighting against creatures called the Firbolgs. The Firbolgs are a giant race with one arm, one leg and one eye. The battle seems to go on and on but in super speed. The passage of time is hard to tell. Suddenly the Firbolgs are few and the tall, fair people rule the land. The sun is shining on the lush green trees and grasses. Peace settles upon the land.

I look at Avalon to see her reaction. She is staring at the tall, fair skinned people completely enthralled. I get up and walk behind her and kneel down.

"Those people are the Tuatha De Danann." I whisper to her.

"How is this possible?" She asks.

"It is one of my gifts." I confess.

"You have more than one too?" She looks at me questioningly.

"Yes."

The scene before us changes again. The sky is lit up with lightning and we plunge into semi-darkness. From the east come another people of dark hair that harness strong magic. They fight against the fair ones and drive them away from their homes to a large hill. A large man with red hair commands the other fair ones to join him. As they gather together at the top of the hill the lightning flashes brightly. The lightning stops and the fair ones are gone.

I walk back to where I was sitting before. The lights brighten back up and the walls of the living room are visible.

"That. Was. Amazing!" Avalon looks at me wide eyed and then her face clouds in confusion.

"I don't understand what I saw," Avalon confesses.

"What you saw was the Tuatha De Danann. Their history of how they conquered Ireland and lived in relative peace and harmony until the Milesians drove them away." I explain.

"They weren't driven away, they vanished!" Avalon exclaims.

"No, the Dagda, the man with the red hair. He was able to move his people to a different plane of existence, another realm. He moved them to a place outside of our time, but is still on this earth. It is called the otherworld by humans. It is really called the Sidhe." I look around the room and see Carl still looks like he is going to be sick.

"The Sidhe? What is that?" Nickolai looks at me in confusion.

"The Sidhe is not just the name for the otherworld but also the name for the people that live in it." I explain.

"But what happened to the Tuatha De Danann?" Avalon asks, clearly excited about the fair people.

"Avalon, the Tuatha De Danann rule the Sidhe." I smile at her.

"What kind of people live there?" She asks quickly.

It's almost as if she is soaking this all up like a sponge. Like a little girl does with a new fairy princess story.

"Oh all kinds, and not just people. There are Leprechauns, Fairies, water Nymphs, wood Nymphs, Brownies, Unicorns, I could go on and on. The Tuatha De Danann invited the Fae and unique creatures to live with them for protection against those that would wish them harm."

"But if all the Fae live there how are there people here that have their abilities?" Nickolai interrupts.

"Some Fae did not wish to leave their homes. Some Fae come back to this world during Samhain, when the veil to the Sidhe is easier to pass through. The Fae have tendencies to mate with humans and then leave. The offspring is then left with the human parent." I shrug.

"There is another reason as well." Carl finally speaks.

"I think we should save this for tomorrow, some of us have been up over twenty four hours now. Avalon looks like she is about to pass out right here." Nickolai looks at Carl and me.

"I'm pretty sure that the rest can wait a few hours for some sleep?" Nickolai asks.

I nod.

CHAPTER 17

Avalon

I wake to a coldness that seems to seep into my bones.
I sit up, rubbing my arms trying to warm myself. I look around
me. There is a muted light coming from a small candle sitting
on a table in the corner of what looks to be a room cut out of
rock. Between me and the desk looks like iron bars. I am back
in the cell!

I do not know how I got here. I think back and
remember that I went to bed at my dad's house after seeing
Rion again in such a long time. Rion seems different, maybe
the time at the boarding school has done him some good. I
shake my head of my thoughts.

"This is just a dream, it's not real," I tell myself.

"Oh this is no dream, it is definitely real." A voice
comes from the robed figure that is sitting at the desk.

I panic. No one has ever talked to me in my dream

before. The voice seems familiar but I can't place where I know it from.

"Why am I here? What do you want with me?" I demand

"Oh I think you already know why you are here. It's not what I want with you. Someone else is very interested in you." The figure shudders a bit and shakes its head. "Enough, no more questions. You will be made presentable to him soon."

The figure stops speaking and a quick loud knock sounds against the steel door of the room. The robed person gets up, still facing away from me and opens the door. Two women come through the doorway carrying a white cloth, a bucket, and soap. The figure goes back to the desk and continues writing something.

One of the women, the one with the dark hair, unlocks the cell. I try to run, but the shackles I hadn't noticed before stop me. Where did those come from?

"It is no use running anyway, you wouldn't get far. The chains are just so we don't have to chase you down." The woman with the dark hair says with a smirk.

"She doesn't look like she is as dangerous as he believes she is." The red haired one states smartly.

"It's not our business to question, just get her ready." The brunette snaps at the red head.

I'm quickly stripped of my clothing. The women are washing me with cold water from the bucket with the hard bar of soap. If I was cold before, I really didn't know what cold was, until now. I can't keep my teeth from chattering. My whole body is shaking from the cold.

The brunette pulls the white cloth over my head. When she is finished, I notice I'm wearing a white dress that has a square neckline. It has long form fitting sleeves and a bodice that hugs my body before the rest of the dress flows down my legs. The red head fixes my hair while the brunette holds me in place.

The women leave me as quickly as they came in. The brunette stops by the table for a moment.

"She is ready, don't damage her bringing her in." The brunette tells the robed figure.

The robed figure stands up and turns toward me. I can't see a face, it's hidden in shadows by the hood. The figure walks into my cell and unlocks the chain from the wall. With the chain in hand the figure begins to walk out of the cell without saying a word. The hand on the chain proves that the figure is a man. I follow him before the length of chain becomes taut and causes me to fall.

We walk in silence as he leads me down tunnels cut into rock. We enter into a large room. In front of me is a stage, where a man in a purple robe stands addressing the crowd. Towards the back of the room appears to be a balcony above a large opening to this room. The room is lit with torches and is warmer than my cell was.

I look about the room, I know what is going to happen next. I look for the shining one, the one I hope will save me from this horrible place and what is to come. Just as I am brought before the purple robed man, I spot him. His sandy blonde hair seems brighter, his eyes seem to be glowing bright with a light of their own.

Am I imagining this? Does everyone else see him lighting up the room with his brilliance? I look around and everyone else seems oblivious to him. I look back in his direction, he has a worried look on his face, but he flashes a smile my way. There seems to be a confidence there, or at least I hope so.

The purple robed man stops speaking to the crowd and grabs my right wrist hard. I cry out from the pain. The other robed man releases the shackles from around my ankles. There is a sharp pain on my index finger, and suddenly my finger is in the purple robed man's mouth! I try to yank my hand away. The man starts laughing.

"This one is perfect. The best that I have ever tasted in fact. You have outdone yourself!" The purple robed man looks back at the other robed man that is standing next to the doorway that we entered from.

Tasted? What in the hell? Is this guy a Vampire?

There is a sharp pain and mounting pressure that clamps down on my neck. I didn't even see the man move! The roar of the crowd becomes deafening, and then starts to quiet down. I look around for the shining man. I find him, he is fighting with some of the people with the crowd trying to get to me.

My eyes feel heavy and it's getting hard to breathe. My breaths come shallow and farther apart. I just want the pain to be over. I stop caring what that will mean when the pain stops. The pain vanishes and I try to move but I can't. I try to open my eyes or cry out. I can't do that either. I try to feel my surroundings with my body, or hear something. There is nothing.

~*~

"Avalon!"

A voice calls to me but I can't seem to answer it. I still can't move or speak.

"Avalon!" The voice seems louder, more urgent.

I feel movement, like I'm being shaken. Well that is better than the nothing I felt before. I try to open my eyes and a blurry image of a man comes into view, an image I do not recognize, but the voice sounds familiar. My vision clears and Rion is shaking me.

"Ok!" I croak out.

My voice sounds horrible. I bring my hand up to my throat, surprising myself that I can move again.

I look around the room, I'm in my room again. Dad and Nickolai stand behind Rion. I sigh in relief. I hear a collective intake of breath. Rion grabs my arm and looks at my wrist. Then he looks at my neck. He looks scared.

"What?" I ask Rion

"You have someone's hand mark on your wrist and your neck is bruised!" Rion tells me.

I start to panic. It was just a nightmare. Wasn't it?

"But it was just a nightmare!" I can feel that I'm about

to lose it.

"I don't think it was." Rion said sadly. "Go on and get dressed, we will leave and meet you downstairs. I have more to tell everyone and it doesn't look like it can wait much longer."

The seriousness of his tone scares me. My dad looks at me in worry and then ushers everyone out of my room. I wait for everyone to leave before pulling down the covers to get out of bed. My legs are sore. I look down and find a singular red ring around each ankle. I start to cry. A smell lingers in my room and it steals my attention away from myself.

It smells familiar, of sandalwood, musk and jasmine. It is the same smell from my room in my apartment! That time when I felt the arms of someone comforting me on my bed. I smile, remembering how panicked I was, it was just my brother. I laugh a little to myself. The fact that he came to me to comfort me when I needed it made me feel warm inside. He always knew when I needed something, even when we were kids. It kind of bothers me that he came into my apartment like that. I let the thought slip away.

CHAPTER 18

Rion

Platters of breakfast food line the counter. Even though it is three in the afternoon, this is when everyone is starting to wake and join the living. I pick up pancakes, eggs, bacon and sausage and walk toward the kitchen table. I sit down across from Avalon, while Nickolai helps a severely wounded man to the chair at the end of the table. Next to me is a red haired woman that is twitching nervously with an empty plate. Her scent is off, she is definitely not human. I'm not really sure what she is but she is very pale with bright blue eyes.

"Anyone want to start up the introductions again?" I look pointedly at Avalon who was starting to dig into her plate of food.

"Sorry. Rion, this is Drew, he works with me at CommTech." She gestures to the man at the end of the table. "Melanie is the one sitting next to you, she also works with me." She nods over at the red head's direction.

"Wait, Melanie. Not the same one?" I ask Avalon.

"Yes, the same. It doesn't matter now." Avalon quickly dismisses the direction the conversation is starting to turn.

It makes me wonder what changed to make her not want to let Melanie know how she affected Avalon before. I don't press. Avalon must have a reason.

I look to Drew. "So what happened to you?"

Drew looks at Avalon, then to Nickolai who shakes his head. "Well that is hard to say, I don't really remember."

I look around at the people at the table. Avalon, Nickolai, Drew and Melanie are all staring down at the table. I know they are hiding something. They all look so guilty but none quite so much as Nickolai and Melanie. I leave it be for now, we can get into it after we eat.

Melanie looks extremely uncomfortable, she does not have a plate in front of her nor is she making a move to get any food. I will not pry as I don't know her. Maybe she is fasting for reasons all her own. I catch a faint scent of what smells like old blood. I look around for the source. Melanie is nervously playing with her hair, as she moves it, a trail of old blood is on her shoulder.

I stiffen in alarm. Is she one of those vampires that the council warned me about? Wouldn't she be with Morcant instead of here? There seems to be many answers I must have, but again, it can wait until we've eaten.

We finish eating and gather in the living room. I pace the floor waiting for everyone to get comfortable.

"So what's going on?" Drew looks around the room in interest.

"I take it no one told you what was discussed last night?" I look at him before looking at Nickolai.

"Oh yeah, Nickolai did when he came to help me out. From what I hear I missed quite the magic show. Is there more?" Drew asks excitedly.

"You could say that." I chuckle to myself. "So the next part that I need to tell you." My voice drifts off as I try to think where to start.

"Do any of you know what changelings are?" I ask.

"My grandmother used to call me one when I was acting up as a child. She always said I had to be fairy born acting the way I did. Isn't that where a fairy baby is switched for a human one?" Melanie says.

She looks at me but her hands don't seem to stop fidgeting.

"Sort of. A long time ago, hundreds of years ago in fact, the people of the Sidhe used to switch their unwanted children with human children. Sometimes being a changeling was a form of punishment given by the Queen because she disliked bloodshed." I inform them.

"How is being a changeling a form of punishment?" Avalon looks at me questioningly.

"When it was used as a punishment the changeling did not start off as an infant, they were at youngest, teenagers. They were magically reformed as infants and their memories stripped. They were then swapped with human babies and the Sidhe raised the humans as their own, yet still beneath them."

"I remember Mom telling me stories that sounded very much like this, what does this have to do with what is going on now?" Avalon crosses her arms and looks at me like I am wasting her time.

"I know what you're thinking. Trust me, I am not wasting your time, there is more. I was told of such a changeling that was sent here to live among humans for something he did against the High King of the Sidhe. Generally, the High King loves nothing better than to dispatch his enemy with the sword. In this case, he did not. This puzzled the council and both courts. When the man was reformed into an infant and given to human parents in exchange for their child the Sidhe courts learned that one of the prized treasures of the Sidhe was also missing." I explain

"Did they think the man stole it? If he was changed into a baby, how could he have hidden it from the rest of the Sidhe?" Melanie finally speaks.

"I asked that question too. According to the histories, the treasure that was stolen was a cauldron. This cauldron could only be controlled by a man. It had the ability to sustain anyone for as long as they lived with food and drink." I look at Melanie.

Drew snorts. "How could a baby hide a cauldron anyway? Aren't they huge?"

"Not necessarily. Cauldrons come in all sizes. This cauldron had other magical properties that allowed it to shrink to a more manageable size. The Sidhe believe that the treasure was stolen by someone else and given to the baby when the switch was made." I try to explain.

"What makes them think this?" Melanie asks.

Melanie looks as though she is about to jump out of her chair at any moment. She is no longer sitting on the chair but crouched upon it. She is making me nervous.

"The Keeper of the Cauldron was found dead at his station. The ruling council found that the person that was supposed to make the switch with the human child was knocked out. Their theory is that whoever killed the Keeper also knocked out the person that was meant to make the switch." I watch Melanie warily.

"I'm sorry but I'm done with fairy tales and stories for now." Melanie stands up, grabs Nickolai and pulls him outside.

CHAPTER 19

Melanie

I've had enough of fairy tales. Sitting in that chair listening to Rion ramble on about nothing consequential is irritating. Especially, when hunger is eating me from the inside out. I pull Nickolai outside to talk since no one else here can help me deal with this. I shut the door a little too hard. I wince. I hope I didn't slam it too hard and cause anything to break.

The sun is thankfully hidden by the mountains but only just. It is still quite light out but the rays won't burn me. I don't need additional pain. I turn around to confront Nickolai on what to do about my situation.

"Nickolai, what can I do to calm this hunger? It hurts so much!" I look at Nickolai for the answers I know he has.

"You have done very well considering you fed last night. The human blood you consumed should sustain you for a week. You aren't used to the pain yet, and that will never go away. I've learned of a few tricks from other Vampires that you can use." Nickolai looks at me with a combination of amusement and irritation on his face.

"What are they? I'll do anything!" I plead.

"Are you sure of that? It almost sounds like you forgot what I told you last night." Nickolai smirks.

I narrow my eyes at him. I want to slap the look off of his face. I didn't ask for this!

"I can't remember the whole conversation. I remember you talking about vegetables and fruit vaguely."

"I know you are vegan, but you are going to have to get over that, and fast." Nickolai smirks.

"What?" I ask in alarm.

"Do you see the squirrels, rabbits and groundhogs out in the fields? Nickolai questions me.

I look out beyond the nicely kept yard and the natural wind break of the trees that make up the property line of the house. The fields are active with all kinds of animals.

"Yes. What about them?" I retort.

"You need to go feed on some of them. Raw meat and animal blood will help lessen the pain you are feeling. It will help with your control around people." Nickolai points out into the fields beyond the yard.

"You're kidding. You expect me to basically eat rodents!" I shudder at the thought of eating small rodents raw.

"Yep. They are tricky and fast little bastards. Eventually you might actually have fun with it. It will also help you learn how fast you can be as well as hone your abilities." Nickolai grins.

Nickolai turns and walks to the door. He looks at me a brief moment and then makes a shooing gesture at me. He turns without another glance and goes inside the house, leaving me outside by myself.

I crumple down to the grass. The only way to curb the pain is to eat rodents raw. The thought makes me want to retch. I sit and close my eyes trying to make myself calm down. When I open my eyes again the sky is darker. A bright orange-pink strip of sky is still visible just above the mountain peaks. The sky itself is mottled blue and purple.

It is quiet out here. There are no sounds of cars or people. The pain has not dulled since I came outside. I know if I don't do something I will go stark raving crazy from pain. I look out to the fields. There is more activity now as more wild life has come out during the night. I watch as a few large birds swoop in and grab small animals from the ground.

I run fast into the field. It's now or never. I go after a rabbit and it darts out of my way at the last second, just as I dive for it. I make a face plant into the long overgrown grass and dirt. Surprisingly it did not hurt but I know that I'm giving everyone else in the house quite a show. I look to the house. There is only one person outside.

Drew is sitting on one of the patio chairs. Someone must have brought him outside for fresh air. It seems like he is always around, at work and now here. It is not an intrusive presence, but it bugs me a bit and I'm not sure why. In the past he has been nothing but nice to me. I shrug it off, maybe this change is just making me irritable at everyone.

I focus on his face to see if he has been watching and laughing at me and my attempts to catch a rabbit. His face is suddenly close up, as if he is right in front of me. His blue eyes focus directly on mine. He smiles, bringing out the cute dimples on his face. I shake my head. I can't believe I just thought that. I look at him again, his face zooms into focus and there is now a golden ring around his pupil; his blue eyes brighter. What the hell is he?

I think back over the last twenty four hours. Drew has never treated me differently after my change. He acts the same around me that he always has. Maybe he isn't such a bad guy after all. I shrug to myself. It doesn't matter now, he stinks like Nickolai does. I can't get past that stink even if I wanted to.

I turn my focus back to the animals nearby. I watch as a coyote in the distance catches a rabbit and goes down on its haunches to feast on its meal. Now that would be a challenge. I grin to myself. I try as hard as I can to be quiet. I circle around the coyote while it is eating, keeping myself downwind from it. I hope the wind doesn't change before I can make my move. A twig snaps just as I'm about five feet away from the animal.

The coyote gets up quickly and turns on me. I must not look all that scary. It leaps at me baring its teeth. I side step the attack. It amazes me how slow the animal is and how fast I'm able to move out of its way. The coyote and I circle around each other. My mouth starts to salivate and I feel my fangs coming down.

The coyote takes another leap. I dodge it again. This

time I clamp my left hand down hard on its muzzle to keep its mouth shut and take it to the ground. I pin the animal down and sink my teeth into its neck. I drink deeply from it. The blood does not taste like the human blood I've tasted. It is not totally disgusting but it isn't as good. I rake my long nails down the under belly of the animal, spilling out its insides.

I dig into the raw meat spread out before me, still warm, but cooling by the second in the evening breeze. I finish what I hope will satisfy me for a while. The pain from hunger has subsided to a mild dull ache. I stand up and check out my clothes. My clothes are full of dirt, blood and stained by grass. I walk back toward the house, I know my face is probably covered with dirt along with my hair, but I feel good. I stretch out my arms wide feeling the pull of my muscles. I twist my neck feeling it pop and releasing the tension I didn't know was there. I haven't felt this good since last night.

The truth of what I did hits me again. My footing falters and I fall to the ground. It doesn't hurt. My heart hurts because of what I did to that poor woman, nothing else matters at this moment.

I hear my name being called which pulls me out of my thoughts. I look up to see Drew struggling to get up out of the chair. The door opens and Nickolai steps out to check on Drew. I see Drew pointing in my direction. I wave to them to let them know that I'm okay. Physically, I'm okay. Mentally, not so much.

I stand back up and try to dust the dirt off myself. I watch as Nickolai goes back into the house and shuts the door. Drew is still sitting on the chair. It seems as if he is waiting for me.

"Get a nice show?" I call out as I approach him. I wince as I hear how nasty that sounds coming out of my mouth. I didn't mean it to come out like that.

"Actually, yes I did. Thanks." Drew quips and smiles at me.

I laugh. I wasn't expecting him to react that way.

"You did very well for your first time. The face plant was especially funny after I knew you weren't hurt."

I looked at him for a moment. The smile is back and a look of sincerity is in his eyes.

"Can you help me back inside? They are waiting for you before they continue. I wanted to get some fresh air and a good view while they took their break." His mouth quirked into a sideways smile at the last comment.

"A good view or they needed someone to watch me?"

"Both. Still it was a good view for me." Drew whispers.

His flirting excites a small part of me.

I sigh. "I don't know if I can get past your stink long enough." I tease him.

"Oh come on, you know you like my stink." Drew laughs.

I laugh. "Oh yes, I just love the smell of rank animal."

"Have you smelled yourself lately? You just drank from a rank animal, you're covered in its stench." Drew laughs at me.

I smell my shirt and then hold it away from my body. How did I not smell that before? My shirt doesn't smell half as bad as Drew and Nickolai but there is a similarity.

"I don't think I could hold my breath that long anyway." I tease him.

"Have you tried?" Drew's tone is serious.

I look at him for a moment. Is he being serious or playing around again? A small part of me hopes he isn't playing with me.

"I don't know much about the abilities you have or will come to have. You never know if the movies got some of it right or not." Drew shrugs.

"I honestly didn't think about it. It didn't occur to me to test holding my breath just because you stink." I poke his left arm. "Come on. I think I can deal with your stench until we get back in the house." I tease.

"Oh thank you, kind mistress." Drew makes a mocking bow as he sits there looking at me.

I laugh.

"It's good to see you smiling and laughing again."

I stop laughing. I blush slightly and did not say anything to him after that. I wasn't too sure how to respond to him.

CHAPTER 20

Rion

The group gathers again in the living room. I pace the floor thinking about how to start of this last bit of information. I'm sure Avalon is curious how I could know all this. I know I'll have to reveal myself today. It is Avalon's reaction that I'm afraid of. What if she hates me after this?

"I know you all must think I'm filling your heads with silly fairy tales." I look pointedly at a freshly showered Melanie.

She blushes slightly and looks down at the floor.

"The information I'm sharing with you is the truth. I wouldn't be sharing this information at all had I not been ordered to do so." I look at them, hoping for understanding and trust.

"Ordered?" Avalon looks at me incredulously. "Who is giving you orders?" She looks alarmed and uneasy.

"I'm under orders by the Sidhe Council to inform you of everything, including the prophesy."

"You mean they are real?" Melanie looks at me in shock.

"What prophesy?" Nickolai stands up in a threatening gesture.

"Calm down. I need to get this out and I need you all to listen to everything. Then if you feel like trying to kill the messenger, so be it." I glare at Nickolai.

Nickolai sits back down and holds Avalon's hand to give her support. Oh how I wish I could stop the jealousy that overwhelms me each time I see them that close together.

"The Prophesy was foretold when I was a boy. It has been ingrained in all of the Sidhe since then." I clear my throat before speaking again.

"A dark son betrays,
Dagda's water abused,
an army is raised,
a war against chaos ensues.

A daughter of two worlds,
whose gifts are rare and many,
treasures to be unfurled,
which cannot be used by any.

Truth, Blood and Courage bind together,
to control what was stolen,
son and daughter battle each other,
the daughter to bind what was broken."

I look at Avalon to see how she is doing with this

information.

"Aren't prophesies supposed to be old and made up hundreds of years ago or something? You and Avalon are only eighteen." Melanie questions me.

Avalon turns from Melanie to look at me. I can see the gears turning in her head. The blowup that I can see coming from her is inevitable. I have to see this out, she has to know.

"Avalon, your mother and I grew up hearing this prophesy. As kids we thought up fantastical ideas about who the daughter the prophesy could be referring to. It was common knowledge that the prophesy was speaking of Morcant as the dark son. The council seems to think you are the daughter that will save us all."

Avalon sits on the edge of the couch. "This doesn't make sense. You are saying you grew up with Mom, but you are my brother."

"Actually, I'm not your brother. My name is Rob." I step back as I tell her this truth.

"What? Where the hell is my brother then if you're not him?" She yells at me.

Carl puts a hand on her shoulder. "Calm down, your brother is fine."

"Wait, you knew about this?" Avalon turns and looks at Carl in disbelief.

"Yes, your brother was sent to live with your mother's parents to safeguard the bloodline, in case something happened to you. I hope that doesn't happen, but Rob came in your brother's place to watch over you."

Avalon stares back at me. "Well you may as well drop the disguise and stop pretending to be my brother. I knew something was off but I thought it was because of Mom's death, not that he was switched!"

I release the glamour, I can feel the shift in the air around me as the illusion of Rion fades. Gone is the stocky boy with short brown hair and hazel eyes. My wavy sandy blonde hair, yellow-green eyes and shimmering skin in all its unsubtle glory is able to be seen by everyone. I wonder what they will think at their first sight of a Fairy.

Avalon gasps in astonishment. I watch her as she takes in my true form. She starts breathing fast and shallow. Her head starts shaking in disbelief. Nickolai and Carl look at her in alarm.

"This is too much!" Avalon blurts out before bolting off the couch and running upstairs.

Her door slams to her room. Leaving everyone in the room just as confused as I am. Nickolai gets up to go after her and Carl grabs his arm.

"No, I will go see Avalon and bring her back downstairs. She can't run from who she is. She needs to know everything." Carl's head dips down. I watch him leave the room and go after Avalon.

CHAPTER 21

Avalon

I couldn't believe my ears! Rion is telling me he is not my brother? This makes no sense, Rion is my twin! The air around Rion shimmers and he begins to shift. His brown hair turns sandy blonde. His body becomes taller and slimmer. Rion's dark hazel eyes start changing color to green and yellow with a silver ring around his pupil. I gasp at the result of the transformation.

The man that stands before me is the same man from my nightmares. The one I always hope is going to save me from the purple robed man! If he is real, then these nightmares are real. I start to hyperventilate. I realize he was in my bed, in my room, in my apartment that day. I feel sick.

"This is just too much!" I manage to blurt out as I leap up from the couch and run for my room. I need to throw up, be alone, something. I just need to be out of this room!

I run up the stairs taking them so fast that it is almost

like I'm flying. I reach my room, open the door and slam it shut as soon as I clear the door. I'm so mad at everyone I can hardly see straight. Nearly everyone has lied to me for the past year or longer. My life feels like it is spinning out of control and I can't seem to find the exit to get off.

I run for the bathroom. I reach the toilet and retch violently. I sink down to the tile floor letting its coolness settle me down. I feel a presence in the room with me. I didn't even hear the door open.

"Avalon, honey. I am so sorry. I wanted to tell you but just didn't know how. I wanted to protect you and to keep you safe. It is one of the reasons we moved to Colorado after your mother's death." My dad takes me into his arms and I can't help but cry.

"The night your mother died she came to me in spirit, warning me to take you and your brother and leave our home. I knew the time had come where who she was had caught up with her. Rob, the man downstairs, appeared that same night. He advised that Rion would need to go to your grandparents for safe keeping since he did not seem to have any gifts other than an uncanny knack of drawing things from the Sidhe. Rob also said that you needed to be monitored for safety and also to see if you possessed the gifts of the prophesy."

"Who is Rob? Why does he have so much say in my life? What makes you think I could possibly be the one this council thinks I might be?" My muffled questions come out.

"Avalon, I can't lie to you anymore. The things I have seen you do all your life. You could be the one the prophesy speaks of. It does not state what the gifts of the one are, but you have already proven you have more than one. As for Rob, all I know is that he is part of the royal guard. He will only have as much say in your life as you allow him to. Remember that."

I nod just as more questions bubble up in my mind.

"How can I save millions when I don't know how to control what I can do or what else I'm capable of. What if I hurt innocent people in the process?" I blurt out.

"Oh my darling daughter. You have such a big heart and I know you are strong enough to achieve whatever it is you are meant to do in this life. Don't give into doubts and fears." My dad hugs me fiercely.

I sniff and wipe my tears away with my hands.

"You seriously think I can do all that on my own?" I look at him incredulously.

My dad looks at me, his eyes leveled at mine. "Do you seriously think we would let you do all that on your own?" He smiles at me after using my own lingo on me. It sounds pretty silly the way he says it.

Somehow I feel a little bit better. The information is still daunting but knowing that I have help lessens the stress of it just a little. I'm not alone. Dad, Nickolai, the man down stairs, Drew, Melanie and who knows how many others will help me when everything goes to shit.

"Get cleaned up and we will wait for you downstairs. I think he has some more to share with us." My dad says as he stands back up and wipes off his pant legs.

I nod. I watch my dad leave my room before bothering

to get up off the floor. I wash my face and dry off with the hand towel next to the sink. I need to know more before I can face this bizarre existence I call a life.

CHAPTER 22

Rob

Avalon sits back down. Her eyes a little red from crying. I hate that I've caused her grief, but I know she needs to know the truth in order to move forward. She looks up at me.

"Please continue. I know there is more to this. What role did my mom have in all of this?" Avalon tells me, her demeanor and tone of voice seems void of emotion.

It's almost scary how much she reminds me of her grandfather. How he can check himself so quickly and gets straight to business with no emotion. Like a wall is put up.

"In our society when a child reaches the age of decision, or eighteen, they choose their direction in life. I assume that growing up with the prophesy constantly on her thoughts is why your mother decided to take the direction she did. When it was her time, your mother requested to go into the changeling program. I believe she thought that since her gift was so unique and rare that her children would inherit her gift. Coming to this realm was the only way to achieve the daughter the prophesy spoke of."

"What was her gift?" Melanie asks curiously.

"Trieva had the ability to touch anyone and acquire their abilities. She was then able to use them at a master level."

"So the only reason she came to mortal earth as you call it was to have a daughter that would inherit her ability to save your people and its treasures?" Avalon looks at me in disbelief.

"I don't know her reasons. I'm speculating at this point. As we grew older, we drifted apart and wanted different things. I do know that her parents did not agree with her decision to go into the program since she was their only child."

"Did they wipe her memories? Did she know where she came from?"

"The program administrator did not wipe her memories. They wanted her to be able to come back if she wanted to. Your mother was placed with a family that was descended from those who assisted in protecting the gateways in which people could access the Sidhe. The protection they provided was not just for the Sidhe but for those that could unknowingly cross through the veil without being prepared."

"Why did they send her alone?" Avalon asks.

My throat tightens. "She was not sent alone, I was assigned to assist her if she ever had need of me."

"Then where were you the night she died?" Avalon yells at me.

"She didn't call for me until it was too late." I shook my head.

The lump in my throat hardens as the memory of Trieva surfaces, making it harder to talk.

"I didn't know what she had been up to during the few weeks before her death. She had stumbled upon a group of people that had Sidhe abilities but were different. She was the one that first told me of the Vampire-like creatures, like Melanie." I croak out.

"When did she talk to you?" Avalon demands.

"The last time I saw your mother, her call had ripped me from the council floor in the Sidhe and I stood next to her in San Francisco. Her body was bloody and broken, she was very close to death." I choke on the last word.

"I'm sorry this is hard for you. You seem to have known my mom pretty well, but I have to know the rest." Avalon pleads.

I nod. Unshed tears hover at the edge of my eyelids from the memory.

"As she drew her last breath a golden light came from her body and split into two separate orbs. One flew off, but the other stayed with me. The orb that stayed changed into the golden shimmering form of your mother. She told me it was now my task to watch over you and that your brother must be sent to her parents. She was the one who told me to switch with your brother in order to keep a closer eye on you."

I look at Avalon, waiting for a response. She sits there staring at her hands in her lap and says nothing.

"Your mother also told me that your father knew everything. Though I did not know that he was being told at the same time I was. Trieva told me that I must take you back to the Sidhe once you reached the age of decision, so that you could learn of your place and could make an informed decision on what you would do. I was planning on taking you back this weekend before all this happened."

CHAPTER 23

Avalon

I don't want to believe what I am hearing. I am supposed to be going with a man I don't know to a place unknown, where my mom supposedly came from. That I am also not mostly human. Having a long forgotten ancestor that wasn't human I could deal with, but my mom? It sounds insane!

I stand up and glare at Rob.

"I'm not going anywhere with you! I don't even know you. All I know of you is that you claim to know my mom and have been pretending to be my brother for almost two years!"

My dad stands up and places a hand on my upper arm that calms me just a bit.

"Avalon, you need to learn about where your mother came from. You need to learn how to use your abilities properly before someone gets hurt because you don't know how to control them." My dad says.

"Can Dad and Nickolai come too? I ask Rob.

"If you all go, what will happen to us?" Melanie looks around nervously.

"You have a lot of training and education to attend to when you go, you won't have time for a boyfriend." Rob looks pointedly at Nickolai who bristles visibly at the offense. "Your dad can come because he is family."

Rob telling me what I will and won't have time for irritates me further. It seems as if Nickolai can sense my irritation as he places a hand on my forearm.

"I need to get clarification here." Nickolai speaks up. "Was Avalon's mother a Merrow?"

"No she was not. Avalon's Merrow traits are from her father."

Nickolai swears under his breath. "So you are saying that she has inherited Fae traits from both her parents?"

"Yes, it's the natural order when it comes to our kind, though of course there have been times when our kind seeks comforts from humans."

I gasp remembering what Nickolai told me before about Morcant feeding off of Fae.

"Why does this information sound like it is a problem?" Rob looks at Nickolai and then me with worry on his face.

"Because it is." Nickolai sighs.

"Explain." Rob commands.

Nickolai bristles at the command but seems to let it slide.

"When I was in the service, I met a man that offered me what I thought would be a better life and a chance to help others once I got out. I jumped at the chance and he Awakened me the next day."

"Awakened?" Rob looks at Nickolai in shock.

"That's what we call it, we have no other term. I found I descended from a tribe that could shift into Were-Tigers. The man that changed me, his name is Morcant."

Alarm widens Rob's eyes. "No."

"No?" Nickolai questions him.

"Morcant is the name of the Sidhe that was made into a changeling as punishment, he is the one we think stole the cauldron. How did he Awaken you?" Rob asks in a hurried tone.

"He used a vial of glowing blue water. Like we use on everyone that we find that has some Fae or Were heritage."

Robs face turns red with anger. "What do you mean we?" Rob demands as he advances on Nickolai.

I stand up to stop Rob. For some reason I know he will stop for me. "Let him explain." I place my hand on Rob's chest, and he seems to calm down slightly.

"You know and you're siding with him?" Rob looks down at me. The expression on Rob's face ranges from anger, to hurt and then confusion.

"Yes I know. He told me once he found out that he had not been able to save me from the Awakening." I tell Rob.

"What?" Rob's voice becomes very loud.

Rob scrutinizes me carefully but seems to calm slightly.

"I was organizing the operation here in Colorado. Once I met Avalon, I tried to keep her out of it, but I was unable to. I didn't want to organize this as I was given no choice, if I refused I would have been killed. I know it's a poor excuse for what I did to so many people, but I did it to save my own neck." Nickolai hangs his head down in shame.

"We all have regrets and mistakes in our past. As long as we learn from them and try to correct them, that is what matters." My dad tells Nickolai.

"That is what I want to do now. After learning so much about what I didn't know before." Nickolai says looking to my dad and then to Rob. "I even have a vial with me that will prove I am telling the truth."

Nickolai removes a black cord from around his neck. A small vial that contains glowing blue liquid dangles from it. Nickolai hands the vial to Rob.

"How much is given to each person?" Rob asks worriedly.

"Just a drop. Morcant wanted them to have access to their abilities but not to be too strong. If we knew that there was no Fae or Were heritage in a young person, that person was given a drop of the water and a drop of Morcant's blood. That is what creates the Vampires like Melanie."

Rob seems to sigh slightly in relief. "Then there is a chance. How many of these operations have been done?" Rob hands the vial back to Nickolai.

"The one in Colorado was the second. The other one hit the news as cult related mass suicides. The bodies that are left behind are the casualties from such an operation. It is when the new ones like Melanie come out of their Awakening and can't control themselves." Nickolai's voice trails off for a moment as if in thought.

"Why are you saying there is a chance?" Nickolai looks inquisitively at Rob.

"This is the same water we use in our ceremonies, the ones that bring out the maximum potential in our abilities. We normally use the whole amount that is in this vial per ceremony." Rob explains.

"How do you have access to the water if the cauldron was stolen so long ago?" Drew asks.

"Because we saved the water in a special cask used only in ceremonies, though it is now getting low."

I then realize Rob did not say that Nickolai could come with us.

"Why can't Nickolai come with us?" I look defiantly at Rob.

"Because magical mutations are taboo." Rob looks sternly at me.

CHAPTER 24

Rob

"What do you mean taboo? What magical mutations?" Avalon fires back.

"Avalon, if your father was not also Merrow, he wouldn't be allowed to come either, family or not. It is just not done."

"What do you mean also? What isn't done?" She demands.

"Avalon, you are not just Sidhe and Merrow. You carry the genetic mutation though you can't access it, of a Were-Panther." I tell Avalon.

"A what?" Avalon looks at me like I have two heads.

"I guess I need to explain how Weres came to be." I sigh and look around the room. It appears both the Weres in the room are oblivious to their own origins.

"The Cauldron has another use though not widely shared with anyone. Yes it has the ability to sustain life with food and drink. It also has the ability to create new life, well, alter life I should say."

"Alter life? What does that mean?" Drew asks.

"A long time ago the Sidhe council decided to gift certain people abilities beyond normal humans. These humans were protectors of the earth and most lived a nomadic existence." I inform them.

"You mean Indians." Drew calls out.

"Yes, that is the term you are familiar with. These people were given a small amount of water and were told to combine it with the blood of any animal they thought would best serve to protect the earth and have their fiercest warriors drink it. These warriors were changed from the day they drank the potion. Their male descendants also could change into the new form, the females could not." I explain.

"So that is why I'm a wolf and Nickolai is a tiger?" Drew looks taken aback.

"That is exactly why." I nod.

Nickolai takes a sharp inhale of breath. Every head in the room turns to look at him including mine.

"What is it?" Avalon asks.

"Morcant was always talking about finding one that had descended from more than two distinct Fae. He was under the belief that if he could find one that is like that, he could drain them of their life blood and then he be immortal. He wants this so that he would no longer need to hunt for more Fae to sustain his life. With Avalon's heritage it makes her the prime target when he finds out about her." Nickolai stated in a panicked tone.

"Then we will leave in two days time, when the gateway is easier to open." I look at Carl and Avalon. "We can't afford for Morcant to find Avalon."

"You still didn't explain why they can't come?" Avalon looks at me. Her stance straightening and her head held high. For a moment she reminds me of her grandmother.

"They can't come because their kind was created to guard our gateways and protect nature. It was never intended for them to pass through the gateways." I point at Nickolai and Drew.

"Besides, in his condition, Drew will just slow us down." I explain.

"What about me?" Melanie asks.

"Your kind are considered abominations. My kind would try to kill you on sight. It is for your own protection that you do not go."

I see the same stubborn look set in on Avalon's face that used to show up on Trieva's face. I knew this is not going to be the last conversation we will have on this topic.

CHAPTER 25

Nickolai

This time she comes at me and I side step her easily before swatting her backside with my large front paw. She loses her balance and goes flying to the ground. I turn and face her and wait for her to get back up. Her face is flushed, just slightly red. She looks a bit angry. Did she really think I would let her pin me this time?

Melanie comes at me again but instead of going straight for me, she side steps and then jumps over me trying to catch me off guard. It works but I am quick to adapt. She tries to grab me around the ribs to crush me down to the ground. I turn quickly and ram against her knocking her to the ground. Just as I am about to bring my mouth around her throat for her to concede I hear Rob congratulating Avalon on something she did. I look at them and notice Rob is no longer sitting in front of Avalon, but is behind her, with his hands on her shoulders and he is slightly rubbing them.

I growl. Suddenly the world flips upside down and I am flat on my back again, Melanie's hand clamped down around my throat, her body pinning mine down. I snort. Melanie laughs.

"It's what you get for letting yourself get distracted." Melanie teases me.

I shift back and stand up, dusting the dirt and grass from my body. "Yeah, yeah."

"I can see you're not into this anymore, and I need to eat before the sun comes up."

I barely acknowledge that she said anything as I walk towards Avalon and Rob. Rob stands up and dusts off his knees. There is a cup in front of Avalon that appears to be boiling without a heat source.

"Avalon that's enough for right now. Controlling temperatures is difficult work. You are off to a good start now that you can bring water to boiling and shape it. Next you will need to learn how to freeze it. For now, it is time to eat. It's fajita night!" Rob smiles and sighs like he is in heaven at the thought of fajitas.

I start to chuckle. The meat is smelling really good now. Rob reaches down to Avalon and she takes his hand as he helps her to stand up. They turn to face the house and find me standing there.

"Oh, how long have you been waiting for me?" Avalon looks at me. There is a slight flush to her cheeks.

My jaw clenches. From what I see, it looks like she is reacting to Rob's touches.

"I just got done with Melanie." It isn't what I want to say but I don't want to come off sounding like a Neanderthal-type jerk.

I reach out for her hand and she steps up to take mine. Maybe I am over reacting to something that isn't there. I wrap her hand up around my forearm and walk with her into the house leaving Rob to follow us.

CHAPTER 26

Avalon

I smile as everyone gathers around the table for dinner. I haven't had a dinner like this since before my mom died. I catch my dad's eye and he smiles back at me and nods. This is nice. The plates of steaming steak and chicken with onions and peppers make my mouth water.

I look down the table and spot Melanie sitting next to Drew with a large hunk of raw steak on her plate. I am glad she was able to join us but secretly glad she is sitting down there where I don't have to watch her eat that. I shudder at image that comes to mind with that thought.

Silence fills the air as everyone is devouring the food on their plates. I'm surprised that I'm as hungry as I am. In the last twenty-four hours I have never eaten so much in one day before. The peaceful silence is interrupted when my cell phone starts ringing. I dig my phone out from my back pocket and look at the caller ID. It's Tripp!

"Hey Tripp!" I answer the phone as I always do when he calls.

"Avalon are you ok? Where are you? Have you seen the news?" Tripp rattles off so many questions at once.

"Yeah, yeah, I am fine. Calm down. I'm at my dad's. No, I haven't seen the news." I look in alarm at everyone at the table.

Rob gets up from the table and goes into the living room, picks up the remote and turns on the TV. He changes the channel to the local news and four faces are being displayed on the screen. My face along with Nickolai's, Melanie's and Drew's stare back at us. The pictures look like our work badge photos.

"Shit!" Nickolai drops his fork on his plate.

The words, Persons of Interest, is displayed above our photos.

"Avalon, I am scared. I've been told that people are dead at work, I was afraid you were one of them when you didn't answer your phone earlier and you weren't at your apartment."

I move my phone away from my face and look down at it. There is a missed call. I'm surprised I didn't notice it before.

"When I saw the news I knew you weren't dead so I thought I would try to call you again. Can I come stay with you guys? I don't feel safe out here."

"How long have our faces been flashing up on the news

like this?" I ask Tripp.

"This is the third time I've seen it. There is security footage that shows the four of you leaving work from a side door around two in the morning! What happened? Why were you at work that late?" Tripp's voice is in full panic.

"It's a long story, one I will share with you when I see you. Can I call you back in five minutes?"

"Sure. But please call back, I do not want to be by myself right now."

I hang up the phone and look around the room. This situation has just gotten ten times worse.

"Tripp is back home and is in a full-fledged panic. I think we should have him come here."

"No one comes here. Someone can go get him and bring him here but no one is to tell him where this house is. Understood?" Rob looks at me with a stern look.

"I should be the one to go get him. He will not get into the car with Melanie or Rob, he might get into the car with Nickolai. There is another reason I need to go. I need to go pick up some clothes at the apartment. I am sure Melanie would like to wear something else than what she has worn for the last forty eight hours. My clothes are starting to get stiff from dirt and sweat. It's gross." I complain.

"I agree with Avalon, she should be the one to get him. We can't leave him unprotected. If we do, Morcant's people will use him as leverage to get to Avalon. Also, she is starting to smell almost as bad as Melanie." Nickolai winks at me.

I slap him playfully.

Nickolai laughs then quiets down. "Besides, I need to go down to the police station to clear us. Drew is in no shape to go, and I don't trust Melanie's control yet around normal people."

"I will come with you." Rob tells Nickolai.

"Alright." Nickolai agrees.

"Avalon, you will take my car to go get Tripp, do not go back to your work to get your car. Carl, can I borrow your car tomorrow?" Rob looks to me then to my dad.

My dad nods. "You know where the keys are."

I find it somewhat funny that my dad still treats Rob like he is a kid when Rob is more than likely older than he is.

I dial Tripp's number and listen to the phone ring. He picks up the phone on the second ring.

"Avalon?"

"Yeah, it's me. Look I will come pick you up in four hours, be ready with a bag packed. I would come sooner but I'm exhausted. I need sleep. After I come get you, we need to go to my apartment to get some clothes for Melanie and me. Then we will come back to my Dad's."

"Okay. I am just dying to know why Melanie is there with you. You can fill me in on all the deets when you come get me."

"Ok. See you soon." I hang up the phone. I'm not as hungry as I was earlier. My stomach is now tied in knots.

CHAPTER 27

Rob

Nickolai and I leave in Carl's black Honda Ridgeline after watching Avalon drive away in my blue Ford Focus. I drive us into Greeley and park in front of the police station on 10th Avenue. I have never been to this station, nor ever wanted to be here. All the metal here makes me feel uneasy. The glass walled entry way keeps it from feeling closed in. We walk into the lobby and go to the main window. Nickolai tells the officer behind the glass barrier who he is and that he wants to make a statement. The officer looks up and immediately recognizes Nickolai from his photo.

"I will buzz you in. The officer behind the door will escort you back."

A buzzing sound fills the air as the locking mechanism is being released. The door opens and I move to follow Nickolai.

"Just him, you can wait here." The officer informed me

pointing at the chairs in the lobby.

"The detective will want to speak with me as well." I reply.

"I will talk to the detective. If he wants to speak with you, I will come back and get you."

"I will be going in with him." I inform the officer, my eyes leveled at him.

"Yes, you should come. Follow me please." The officer states, his eyes glassy.

We enter through the large metal door and follow the officer down the hallway.

"Impressive Jedi mind trick." Nickolai whispers with a slight chuckle.

I grin. "Oh just wait, that was nothing."

The officer leads us through two double doors into a room with several desks both empty and occupied. There is a short, portly man sitting at the desk we are brought to. He is busy pecking at his keyboard with two fingers. His coffee is in a stained mug next to the keyboard. There is a half-eaten, chocolate covered donut sitting on a napkin beside it. The nameplate on the desk read, Det. Miller.

The detective looks up and instant recognition shows on his face.

"Who is this guy and where are the girls and the other guy?" The detective demands.

"Drew, the other guy, was in need of medical attention,

he is currently resting at home." Nickolai explains.

"There is no record of Drew being admitted to the hospital, I checked all the people that came in, none of them matched his description."

"Drew refused to go to the hospital. He had me set his bones and wrap him up."

The detective opens a file with Nickolai's name on it.

"Eight years in the navy. I am surprised you didn't go career with that much time under your belt. Field medic?"

"No, but I did have some training, sir."

"The girls?"

"Avalon has a rare medical condition and her father distrusts hospitals so we took her home. Melanie is sick, and has gone a bit crazy, besides, she doesn't talk anymore." Nickolai tells the detective.

I almost don't cover up my smirk in time, with all the lies Nickolai is spewing. The detective looks over at me.

"Who is he?" Detective Miller asks Nickolai.

"His name is Rob, he is Avalon's cousin and was at the house when we arrived after escaping the building." Nickolai responds.

"Do you have any idea what happened in there? What caused all this? The officer questions Nickolai.

"No sir, I blacked out for a while and when I came to the entire office had gone crazy. I was able to find Avalon, and we found Drew trying to hide in a corner after being wounded, and ran into Melanie right before we got to the exit."

I know the questions are going to get more intense, so I start to work my magic. I don't want Nickolai saying anything more in case he accidently gives too much information. I look at the detective and place my hands on his desk. He looks over at me making direct eye contact with me which is exactly what I want.

"You should have what you need now, you have no further questions. It is obvious they were victims and trying to escape. Nickolai, Avalon, Melanie and Drew are no longer persons of interest. They are survivors. You will close this investigation with a plausible explanation such as a bizarre cult ritual."

My eyes flash white as I end my speech. It always happens when I use this much mind control on a human. Detective Miller blinks and then closes his file.

"Ok, we are done here. I am glad you and the others were able to make it out safe. You can go." Detective Miller waves us off and goes back to his paperwork.

Nickolai and I stand up and walk toward the double doors.

"Don't ever use that on me." Nickolai leans over and whispers. "If it wasn't for the white flashy thing you did, I think I would have to start calling you Yoda!"

We both laugh as we exit the station and walk toward the car. I never tell him that I won't use that ability against him.

CHAPTER 28

Avalon

I pull up to the curb outside of Tripp's apartment. Tripp closes and locks his door and picks up the duffel bag he threw on the ground. He turns around I notice he is carrying a Starbucks coffee tray. My hero! I so needed that pick me up this morning.

Tripp opens the passenger door and throws his duffel bag in the back seat. I wait for him to sit down and buckle his seat belt.

"Next stop, my apartment for some new clothes!" I call out as I buckle my seat belt.

"Thank God. No offense girl, but you stink!" Tripp replies waving a hand in front of his face.

"Gee, thanks a lot!"

I stick out my tongue at him. I grab the coffee that has

my name on it and pull away from the curb.

"You're a lifesaver!" I raise my coffee and sip at the hot liquid inside, the sweetness of the cream and caramel hits my tongue and I'm in heaven.

"So are you going to fill me in on what happened or are you going to make me wait until we get to your dad's?" Tripp looks at me impatiently.

"From what I was told, many of us were given something in our coffee. Some of us changed and some didn't. Those that didn't, well most of them did not last long, even some that did change didn't survive. Our boss, Neville, he died too. It was kind of gross."

"Gross?"

"He was in the process of changing into a Leprechaun."

"Say what? Are you pulling my leg? If you don't want to tell me just say so." Tripp huffs in the seat, folding his arms across his chest and pouting.

"I am telling you! Nickolai, well he actually organized this whole thing. He was working for some really bad guy that likes to eat people."

"What the hell are you still doing with him?" Tripp looks at me like I am crazy.

"Well he didn't have much choice. He said he either did it or he would have been killed. He did it to save his own neck, but he feels really bad about it now. He said he even tried to keep me out of it. Which he did, I had two cups of coffee given to me. Supposedly the first one had nothing in it, but it got spilled. The second one, I wasn't so lucky."

I dodge Tripp's actual question. Am I still with Nickolai? I really don't know, our relationship feels different somehow. I'm not even sure when it changed. I still care about him. But the attraction I felt for him before all of this happened as faded a bit.

"What do you mean?" Tripp asks, breaking me out of my thoughts.

"The second one I got had whatever it was in it. It affected me along with others that drank what was in theirs. Melanie turned into a Vampire."

Tripp laughs out loud. "Well that fits, she was always evil. Bad karma, a vegan changing into a Vampire! Priceless!"

Tripp turns in his seat as I park in my spot at my apartment complex. "So what did you turn into?" He seems intrigued.

"I didn't change much." I show him my hands and point out the slight webbing that is now in between my fingers. I take off my sunglasses so he can see my eyes.

"You changed a little bit. Your eyes are the most noticeable. Have you found out what you are?"

"Some, it is confusing though. I'll tell you the rest when we get inside."

We walk up the sidewalk and up the flight of stairs to my door. I go to put the key in the lock when I notice my door is not fully closed. I step back. Tripp looks at me in confusion.

"I remember locking this door when I left." I explain

with panic in my voice.

"How long has it been since you were last here?"

"Three days."

"You know it could have been the police when they were looking for you, and the door just didn't get shut all the way." Tripp tries to calm me down. He pushes on the door and it swings open.

I wait to make sure nothing is going to jump out at me. With all the weirdness happening lately, I never know what to expect. Tripp walks in the apartment and looks around.

"Ok chicken, you can come in now!" Tripp calls out to me.

"Oh shut up! If you had been through what I have been through in the last few days you would be just as freaked out as I am." I smack him on the arm as I pass him.

I walk into my room and grab a duffel bag from the closet. I dump the duffel bag on my bed. I open my dresser and start piling clothes into the bag.

"So are you going to leave me in suspense or are you going to tell me the rest?" Tripp calls out from the living room.

"From what I have been told, my mom came from a place called the Sidhe, my dad descended from some Weres and Merrows, or Mermaids I guess. Supposedly that's why I didn't change much."

"So do you have all kinds of neat abilities now?" Tripp asks as he stands in the door way.

"You sound like you believe I'm making this crap up."
I look at him. Tripp is leaning back against the door frame with
his arms crossed.

"Well it all sounds pretty unbelievable." Tripp shrugs.
"I guess I'll believe it when I see it."

"Go get me a glass of water then. I'll show you." I
challenge him.

Tripp leaves and comes back with a glass of water. I
start to will the water out of the glass. It leaves the glass in a
controlled stream, almost like a live worm. It moves through
the air and wraps itself like a ring in front of Tripp's face.

"Whoa!" Tripp stumbles backwards in surprise. "That
is awesome!"

I put the water back into the glass that he is still
holding.

"Enough of the show. I need to get a few more things
and then we can go."

I turn and walk to the closet and bend down to get a
couple pairs of shoes. I stand back up and suddenly feel
woozy. There is a sudden pain on the back of my head. The
floor starts rushing up to meet me as I lose my balance.
Everything around me goes dark and I can't hear a thing.

CHAPTER 29

Nickolai

I walk back into Carl's house after Rob. I am anxious to see Avalon, to tell her how Rob managed to Jedi mind trick the officer at the front desk and the detective. I walk into the living room to find Carl and Drew watching the Red Sox play against the Yankees. I walk to the back door and open it, hoping to see Avalon out in the backyard enjoying the sunshine. No one is outside.

I close the back door and sit down on the chair. I sigh. Rob looks at me and rolls his eyes.

"Nickolai, I am sure Avalon is fine. We weren't gone that long. Besides she isn't the fastest when it comes to getting things done. She is probably still sifting through her clothes with one hand while nursing a caramel macchiato from Starbucks in the other." Rob tells me while doing a lame impersonation of Avalon.

I laugh. "You would have been one sexy chick." I

tease him. He is acting more like an extremely effeminate man impersonating a girl at this point.

"Wouldn't I though?" Rob fired back, joining in the fun. His face twists up funny as he tries to keep a straight face after that.

I laugh again. "Thanks, I needed that."

Rob nods and walks into the kitchen. He opens the fridge and grabs two water bottles. He tosses one to me.

"Let's get some work done to pass the time. Pick whichever form you want to use and let's have at it." Rob calls out as he walks to the back door.

I follow after him. Getting some frustration out against him will be good. With what I felt last night between him and Avalon, he deserves it.

I barely give him time to set down his water bottle before I shift and charge at him. Suddenly he is not where he was a moment ago. I scramble to stop myself and turn but I trip and go down onto the ground, all limbs flailing wildly. Well that was graceful.

Rob laughs. "I have my own tricks you know." He grins down at me.

How the hell did he disappear? I sniff the air and circle him. He pivots keeping his eyes on mine. I detect a change in the air and suddenly he is gone again. I look down at the grass for movements but I see none.

I sniff the air; the smell of him still lingers in the exact same spot he was in before he disappeared the second time. I walk slowly toward that spot, sniffing the air to see if his scent changes direction. I come close to the spot where he was and turn my head to listen. I hear nothing but his smell is stronger, one of my whiskers brushes up against something that I can't see. I pounce straight ahead and pin down a laughing Rob.

"Good job. Most use sight and sound. You used smell and touch in addition to the others. I am harder to track when I am moving, but the smell, if you know what you are looking for, will leave a trail to follow." Rob grins.

"That is if I haven't masked my smell." He added in.

~*~

Melanie comes outside and I'm impressed on how quickly she is gaining control of her abilities and the shorter sleeping periods. I shift back to my human form and invite her over to spar with Rob and myself. She accepts and joins us in the grass. I remind her to keep her nails under control so as not to draw blood. Melanie nods. I shift back to begin our exercises.

We begin two against one, of course I opt to go first. It was easy enough working with Rob with smell. With two it is harder to concentrate and split my senses between them. I keep my eyes on Melanie, watching her body language and the positioning of her feet. I learned in the service that the body and foot position generally will give away the next action. Rob slips to the side and disappears but I can still detect him off to my right.

Melanie lunges for me and I dart forward, the sound of bodies colliding behind me, makes me stop short. I turn around and see Rob on top of Melanie who is busy eating dirt.

She jumps up abruptly knocking Rob off of her, spitting grass from her mouth. Rob goes crashing into the grass again, arms flailing. The sight was so funny, I lost my focus and shifted back into human form. I laugh so hard tears start to form in my eyes.

We go through another three rounds of this alternating who will be up on deck on two to one. I am about to go in for the win when Carl throws open the back door and runs over to us.

"Has anyone heard from Avalon? She is not home yet and I don't have Tripp's number," Carl says in a panic.

I look around. I swear to myself. How could I have been so blind? The sun is already on its downward journey but not quite at sunset that would change the sky and clouds different colors. I shift forms and pull my cell out of my back pocket. I dial Avalon's number, it rings three times then goes to voicemail and her sweet voice comes on telling me to leave a message.

"Avalon, call me as soon as you get this. Hopefully you haven't lost your phone or anything. I will call Tripp after this."

I hang up the phone and scroll through my contacts, thankful that I had bothered to grab his number from the employee database before everything went down. I dial the number. A message comes on stating that the number is disconnected. I swear and everyone looks at me.

"The number the company had for Tripp is disconnected. We can only hope that Avalon calls back or that we reach her in another attempt," I explain.

CHAPTER 30

Avalon

The sounds of a chain rattling, a pen scratching on paper, and water dripping brings me out from sleep. The air is cold and the ground is rough and hard. I open my eyes and it is really dark in here. Oh no, not another nightmare. I can't take much more of this, really. I sit up and look around. Sure enough, there are bars to my left, and on the far wall next to the door is a dark robed man sitting at a desk with a small candle as the only light.

My head hurts, I reach up to where it hurts and my hair is matted where something sticky has dried in it. I move to tuck my legs underneath me when a chain rattles and I realize I have a shackle on my ankle. I hear a buzzing sound and look to see where it is coming from. On the desk is my cell and it's vibrating. The man at the desk picks it up and looks at the caller ID. He chuckles slightly and puts it back down.

The man, like in my nightmares, is wearing a dark robe.

His blonde hair is uncovered by the hood on the back of the robe. His hair is closely cut but longer than a buzz cut. I look at him closely and realize only one foot is touching the floor, the other is tucked up underneath him. I shake my head. It can't be.

The man in the chair turns around and looks toward me. His face is in shadows, but I no longer need the light to know who it is.

"Tripp! How could you do this? How are you involved in all this?" I yell at him.

Tripp laughs. "That is not really my name, I have several, but you can continue to use it."

His voice sounds different, deeper and more adult like than the higher tones I was used to. It makes me look at him closer. His perfect hair is disheveled and has no product in it. He is taller than he used to be. Was he always slouching before?

"As to doing this, well, I have been involved in this for quite some time. I am sorry that you turned up to be who you are. I was hoping you would just be able to join our group. To not bring you in, knowing what you are, would mean an existence of servitude."

"Servitude? Why wouldn't Morcant just kill you like he does to anyone else that defies him?"

"I am too valuable to him right now for him to want to kill me. I can see the gears of your mind trying to work out who I could be. Have you figured it out yet?" Tripp grins smugly at me.

The phone vibrates on the desk again. Tripp looks back at it.

"My my, they sure want to find you."

I ignore him and think about what he said before the phone went off. One idea keeps coming to the front of my mind. Something Nickolai mentioned once. The seeker, the one that could locate anyone with Fae or Were heritage. That has to be what he is hinting at, that would make him valuable to Morcant!

"You're the seeker aren't you?" I glare up at him.

"Smart girl. Though a few others will be let in on the secret as well but it will do none of you any good. You won't be in this world long enough to tell anyone that would matter."

"I don't understand how you could have been my friend at all and be so heartless."

"I do what I must to make my life better. I do wish you were not what you are. When I document for Morcant if someone is Were or Fae it is a feeling that I have. It is as if I just know there is something different about them deep down. You were easy to nail down because the feeling was so strong. I had no idea you were exactly what he was looking for. There is nothing I can do about that now and not risk losing opportunities for myself. When friendship gets in the way of my future happiness, the friendship will suffer," Tripp explains.

My cell phone vibrates on the desk again. "Let's answer that shall we?" Tripp grins but the expression on his face seems more evil than his impish tone implies.

CHAPTER 31

Nickolai

I pace the room anxiously as the phone rings in my ear again. I am hoping someone picks up the damn phone at this point, just so I can get some answers. I can barely contain myself in my fear for Avalon. The others try to keep themselves busy but it is pretty obvious from the elevated heart rates in this room that they are all nervous.

The line picks up on the third ring, there is silence on the other end.

"Avalon!" I call into the phone. "Where are you? Are you ok?"

"She is fine, for now." A male but monotone voice answers back.

"Whoever is on the phone, I am in a dark cave that looks like it was part of an old mine!" Avalon calls out in panic. Her voice seems distant, I know he does not have his end on speaker.

I walk back to the table and put the phone on speaker so that everyone can hear but signal them to stay quiet. The phone muffles itself on the other end, as if the man on the other end does not want us to hear what he is saying.

"Who are you? Let me talk to Avalon?"

"You should be able to piece together who I am by now if you stop to think about it. Avalon is fine in her cell at the time being. Unfortunately for her, she won't be in the next forty-eight hours." The voice changes slightly and it almost sounds familiar.

"Is that a threat?"

"I never make threats. It's a promise." The haughty tone in the man's voice finally registers.

"Tripp! What the hell? Why are you doing this?"

"For one thing it is part of my job. You know as well as I do that if I don't bring her in, knowing what she is, I will lose my position with Morcant. I will not allow that."

"Wait. What? You were on the pink list at work!"

"I couldn't have my name left off of the list, it would have been too obvious as I would have fell into one of the criteria for the Awakening."

He had a point, it would have been too obvious.

"Convenient though, that my poor grandmother died and I had to go to her funeral the day before your utter failure." Tripp laughs. "We knew you would not bring her in with the feelings you had developed for her. Plans changed. I just had to sit back and let her come to me. The rest was easy."

I listen while he brags. I listen for what he is not saying. I listen for the sounds around him, what I might be able to recognize. I know he is at a safe house in order to be so smug. Each safe house has cells but there are only a couple in Colorado. Only one that is in an old gold mine.

"Why are you telling me all this?"

"Why? To goad you of course. Even if you are able to figure out where we are, you still will not be able to save her or yourself. You may as well just stay wherever you are and save yourself. We will find you eventually. It is only a matter of time, you know that."

I look around the room at the others. Carl is so red with anger he looks like he is ready to explode. I look at Rob who then looks at Carl and nods his head. Rob gets up from the table and leads Carl out of the room.

"You are very confident you have everything under control. We will see just how confident you are when I get there and rip off your head, you freakish little shit!"

Tripp laughs and ends the call.

"Was your little outburst really necessary?" Drew looks at me with a slight grin.

"Of course it was. He thinks I am a cocky bastard that can handle everything on my own. He is not going to expect me to come with others.

I look to Melanie. "Would you care to join me for a

little revenge? You may not see Morcant but you can take out a few of his followers that would do to others what was done to you without having a second thought."

Melanie grins. "I have been waiting for something to kill and shred."

I laugh. "You are almost ready, some more practice and then I think you will be ready for most of the opposition you will face."

CHAPTER 32

Rob

I pull Carl into the other room before he can give us all away to the man on the phone. I close the door to his study to make sure we are less likely to be heard no matter how loud Carl becomes.

"I want to help! I am done sitting by watching you kids deal with this on your own. I will not let the group of you rescue my daughter while I do nothing. I will not stand for it anymore!"

It takes a lot of restraint not to remind him that I am older than he is. I let him vent.

"I have what it takes in me much more than the others to be able to help. I demand to be given the water so that I can assist in any capacity that my daughter requires!" Carl rants, his arms waving wildly.

I wait to see if he is done. Carl turns and glares at me,

but is silent.

"I believe so as well. We will need to accelerate your training, plus get the water from Nickolai. You won't be as fully Awakened as you should be, but more than those Morcant has been recruiting for his cause."

Carl nods, his arm still crossed in front of his chest. I listen and I can't hear Nickolai or the man on the phone talking anymore. I open the door and motion for Carl to follow. We walk back into the dining room to join the others.

The room feels different, as if all the joy and hope has been sucked out of its occupants. I look at Nickolai and wince as he turns and looks at me. His thoughts are so loud and violent. He notices me wince and his eyes narrow.

"Tell me you had nothing to do with her abduction! You know he will kill her, don't you?" Nickolai yells at me as he quickly approaches where I stand.

"Of course I didn't! I want her alive not dead! She means more to me and my people than she could ever possibly mean to anyone else besides her father." I glare back at him.

We stand face to face, both heated, neither one of us willing to show weakness or back down. Carl comes between us and pushes us back, looking at both of us with a look I know too well. I am acting stupid. I shake my head in disgust, more for my actions than anything else. I have let my emotions get the better of me.

"I am sorry. This is not the time nor the place to have this argument. What we need to do is take action." I apologize to Carl and Nickolai.

"You're right, this is not the time. I am sorry I doubted you." Nickolai looks apologetic to Carl and nods his head at me. "From what I heard during the conversation and not just by what we were told, I know where they are. It will be dangerous, so Carl, I would like you to stay here with Drew."

"What? You can't mean to keep me here when all the fun is going to happen. I want some revenge too!" Drew pipes up.

"In your condition, not being 100%, you would be a liability, not an asset. I am sorry man, but you will stay here." Nickolai looks at Drew.

Drew looks down at the table picking at the papers that lay haphazardly across it.

"Exactly who put you in charge? I am not staying here while some mad men have my daughter. I am going to help. You will give me that water you have so that I may assist at the same capacity you can!" Carl demands of Nickolai.

Nickolai steps back for a moment, as if in shock from Carl's outburst. "I only meant to keep you safe. I don't know how Avalon would handle it if something were to happen to you out there." Nickolai counters.

"She is a big girl. I will be helping and you are not going to be in charge, you are not better than anyone else in this room." Carl's eyes narrow at Nickolai.

I watch as Nickolai stands straighter, his height towering over Carl, not liking his authority to be challenged.

"Enough!" I announce loudly as if I am talking to the guard back home. Nickolai suddenly snaps to attention. I stifle a snicker that is threatening to come out.

"Although you have had military experience and a few years of being what you are now, it does not compare to what I know, nor my experiences. Nickolai, you also need to take more water. What you were given has made you a weak specimen of what you should be. Carl being of Were and Fae heritage will have some unique abilities to bring to the table that you can't. He will be taking most of the water to be close to his full potential. Have I made myself clear?" I look around the room, still in command mode.

Everyone is silent. Drew and Nickolai both have their heads bent slightly to the side. Whether voluntary or not, I know submission when I see it.

"Why didn't I get chosen to take more?" A small voice says.

I look over to the table. Melanie looks straight at me, confusion written all over her face. Then it dawns on me that she didn't speak out loud. She was projecting her thoughts without realizing it.

"Melanie, the reason I am not going to let you take more is because I don't know what it will do to you." Melanie looks at me in shock.

The others in the room all look at me wondering why I said that out of the blue. Oops, I forgot to let everyone else in on that. I chuckle to myself.

"I am sorry, I should have told you this before, but things have gotten out of hand a lot faster than expected. When my people are given the water and Awakened as you call it, we gain the ability of telepathy with other Fae or Weres. It normally does not work with humans, but there are some Fae that do have the rare talent to be able to do that with humans as well. Even though you can't hear my thoughts, when you project yours toward me, I can hear you." I explain to the group as their eyes widen in surprise.

"Melanie, can you please bring me two cups from the kitchen?"

Melanie stands up and nods in my direction before heading to the kitchen.

"So let me get this straight. When you came into the room earlier you could hear what I was thinking?" Nickolai asks incredulously.

"Yep, and you were very loud. That is why I winced. It didn't hurt my ears, it was sharp to the mind. Are you sure you have never had more water after the first time?" I look at Nickolai.

"Unless it was done without my knowledge. Having more than the initial dose was forbidden."

"Well now at least you know why. Had you been given what my people are given, you would have been able to hear Morcant's thoughts. That is, if he was not careful to block you. With no one that powerful around him, he doesn't really need to worry about that."

Nickolai nods. Melanie comes back into the room and puts two small plastic cups on the table. Nickolai hands me the vial he still had hanging around his neck. The liquid inside glows dimly; I only hope it is not a hint of our future. I walk over to the table and pour most of the contents into one cup, the rest is poured into the other.

"I think we better move this outside. I am not quite sure what to expect when Carl takes this." I inform everyone as I pick up the cups and head for the back door.

CHAPTER 33

Nickolai

I assist Drew outside with Melanie helping on his other side. She is being kinder to him. She seems to have moved on from her obsession with me, it is definitely a relief. At least Drew is enjoying her attention. I smile to myself.

Rob places the cups on the patio table. Drew and Melanie sit down next to each other at the table. I stand next to Rob and Carl. I am hoping what I am about to do does not kill me. Experiencing that water the first time was not pleasant, but I am doing this for Avalon and not myself.

"Nickolai, I would like you to take yours first. This way you will be stronger and more able to handle Carl once he goes through his Awakening." Rob looks at me.

I nod my head. "Ready?"

Rob nods. "Whenever you are."

I pick up the cup and down the contents quickly. I back up into the grassy area away from the table as I am not sure what this will do and I don't want to hurt anyone or break anything. I wait for the pain to come, but it doesn't. I feel like an idiot standing here waiting for something to happen. Five minutes pass, I look at Rob and shrug. He looks back at me as if he knows something that I do not.

I start to feel warmer, as if I am under a heating lamp. The heat is getting worse, it's not just my skin that feels warm. I'm on fire! Not really, but it sure as hell feels like it! I close my eyes and drop down to my knees in pain. My hands reach for the ground to steady me. I don't remember pain like this the first time, I don't remember the fire.

As quickly as it came, the pain subsides and leaves me wondering if that was it. All at once it sounds as if someone took a recording of all the wildlife in the area and is now blasting it into my ears. I feel like I am about to retch as all the sound is making me nauseous and my head hurts worse than a migraine. I have never felt this bad in my life. The pressure builds until it is unbearable and I retch uncontrollably onto the grass.

"Focus! Meditate! Calm yourself!" A voice comes into my mind. It is Rob's voice.

I try to shut out everything and just focus on breathing. The sounds start to dim before fading completely out. I back up a bit still on my hands and knees. I'm not sure if I can trust myself to stay upright if I try to stand up. I sit down and try to find my center. The cool breeze blows over my skin and it feels good.

I inhale deeply. Someone smelled sickeningly sweet as

if they had just been bathed in a candy factory. There was a faint smell of ash that went with it. It was not a horrible smell but it was obnoxious. I breathe in again and matched the scent to its owner, Melanie. I could smell the wolf scent that Drew normally carried but it was amplified now. A smell of berries, flowers, and musk was also nearby. Rob. Carl still smelled the same, though his old spice cologne was a bit too much. My nose wrinkles up for a moment. I breathe in again, this time I catch scents of wildlife I didn't recognize out past the property line. I make note of it for later as it will be a good hunt after this is all over.

A calm has settled into my body. No longer do the sounds and smells around me assault me unbidden. I open my eyes to test my next sense. The world looks a lot different than it had before I took the water. Everything is sharper and clearer. I look over toward the nearest stargazer lily that was in the flowerbed near the back door, my vision suddenly zooms in as if I'm looking through a pair of binoculars. I can see every minute detail of the flower down to the small bits of pollen within it.

I stand up and feel stronger as if I'm in the best shape of my life. I wonder what it will be like in my other form. Without concentrating or focusing, my perception suddenly shifts and I'm on all fours looking up at the group. I sit down in shock. I didn't even try to shift and there is no pain!

There is a tingling sensation on my head and I move my front right paw to wipe at my head. That does not make the sensation go away. I shake my head, still nothing. *"You can't swipe me away or shake your head to keep me out."* Rob's voice echoes in my mind. I look at Rob and he is looking at me intently. I look at the rest of the group and they are just looking at me. *"Get out of my head!"* I think back at him. Rob grins and the slight tingling sensation ceases. I shift back to my human form, again void of pain.

"Good, now try to initiate contact with me. I promise not to block your attempt." Rob looks at me as a teacher would his student.

"How?" I'm clueless on what to do.

"Focus directly at me. Do not let anyone distract you. Will yourself to be heard."

Following his direction I look directly at him. *"Can you hear me?"* There is no reaction from Rob. I focus all my attention to him. My eyes focus on his bringing his eyes up close and personal. I feel the slight tingling sensation again. *"Can you hear me now?"* Rob starts laughing. The tingling sensation ceases again. I am not sure why he is laughing. It hits me. I sounded like a Verizon commercial! I bust out laughing.

Carl clears his throat. I'm brought out of my small fit of laughter instantly.

"Sorry, accidental inside joke." I look solemnly at Carl.

Carl nods, walks over to the table and picks up his cup. Before anyone can say anything he downs the contents in the cup. He puts the cup back on the table and walks out into the yard putting distance between himself and the others. I come closer just in case I'm needed. Rob also walks closer to Carl.

"You may want to sit down, this will hit you like a ton of bricks." I warn Carl.

Carl nods and sits down in the grass. After a few minutes, he starts breathing heavier and beads of sweat start popping out on his face. Carl's body goes into spasms and he is laying on the grass shaking violently. Rob and I exchange worried glances. Carl's body keeps fluctuating between extremely hairy with dark brown hair all over, to Merrow form with green hair, webbed hands and feet. The fluctuation is so fast that some of the hair on his body is green instead of just the hair on his head.

It hits me. Unlike Avalon, who was half Sidhe, Carl does not have that to help him control his change. His body is trying to change into two things at once. Maybe he needs to focus on one form so that this does not tear his body apart.

Who knows how the rare ones did this before, maybe that is why they were so rare. I pick the only logical form I can think of, the panther. How do you tell a man to focus on the form of a Merman when he has never seen one before?

"Carl, put all your energy into knowing what a panther looks like. Your body doesn't know what form to take, you need to direct it!" I call out.

I am not sure if this transformation will hurt him or not, since my last transformation was painless. Fur starts erupting all over Carl. The fur is dark, the same color as his hair. The painful expression on Carl's face answers my curiosity. His nose and mouth start to protrude out farther from his face, his body contorts and condenses into the smaller panther frame.

A black panther lies on the grass breathing fast and hard, its eyes still closed. The panther's muscles start to relax and its breathing becomes regular. Gold and silver ringed eyes appear as the lids open up. I am in shock. I have never seen anyone that had eyes like that. Usually someone newly Awakened had either the gold ring around the pupil or the silver, not both.

The panther looks around and is suddenly on his feet. He backs up, trips over his tail causing him to fall backwards. It quickly gets up again and starts hissing. I look at Rob, who nods at me. I shift and move slightly toward Carl, ready to go for him should he try to attack the others. The hissing stops and the panther's head is cocked to the side, its ears twitching. I stop in my approach.

Rob smiles and nods his head. The black panther quickly shifts his feet and quickly launches at me. The panther is not as large as I am and I make a mental note to keep my claws in as I try to bat him away. I'm sure if I was in my human form that the look of shock that would definitely be on my face right now would have the group laughing. My swipe hits the panther's solid form but does not alter his momentum. I lay flat on my back looking up at the sky with a black panther standing on top of me.

I shift back. Carl's weight in his panther form is almost too much.

"Get off." I manage to grunt out.

The panther gets off of me as Rob approaches with a smile on his face.

"I'm sure you enjoyed that." I glare at him

"I did actually. Your face is still expressive in your other form. It was quite humorous seeing your eyes widen so much in surprise when Carl went for you." Rob chuckles.

"*I didn't hurt you did I?*" I look toward Carl and he is staring at me.

I shake my head. "*No, my pride maybe but I'll be fine, I'm a big boy.*"

Carl chuckles. I still feel as if I was ganged up on; I don't like it.

"How is it that he is so strong right from the start?" I look at Rob for an answer.

"You saw his eyes, the distinct color of them?"

"Yes, but that does not answer my question."

"I can only guess that being what he is, that he can draw strength from not just his Were-form but also his Merrow-form at the same time. I wonder if he would be just as strong in his other form, but it would be hard to tell him what to focus on since he has never seen one. That will have to be for later."

"Why doesn't Avalon's eyes look like his? The multi-colored rings?"

"She can never assume the panther form, which is what causes the golden ring. She carries the genes that is all. There has never been a female Were of any species. That is why she only has a silver ring like mine."

I feel an overwhelming urge to take Rob out right when he says 'mine'. It is as if I think he is saying Avalon is his. I need time to myself. I need to run. I'm angry, stressed out and restless.

"I need some time to myself while you train Carl. Grab Melanie to help with any sparring." I call out to Rob as I walk to the edge of the yard. I shift abruptly and take off without waiting for an answer.

CHAPTER 34

Avalon

A sharp rap on the metal door to the room wakes me up. It takes me a minute to remember where I am and why. I look past the bars and at the door to see what I assume is coming for me now. Tripp is sitting at the desk in the corner writing something down quickly before he gets up to open the door.

The door opens up and two women walk through. The tall one has dark brown hair and a silver ring around the pupil of her brown eyes. Her dark skin is smooth and free of any imperfection. The shorter one has red hair, very white skin and bright slightly glowing blue eyes. I make a mental note; one Fae, one Vampire. The tall one carries white cloth in her long arms and reaches out to Tripp and yanks the key to my cell out of his hand.

"Damn Vanessa. You don't need to rip my hand off!" Tripp snaps.

"Don't be so damn slow then. You knew we were coming. We have a job to do and it needs to be done quickly. Morcant will not be happy if she is not made ready on time." Vanessa retorts.

Tripp glares at Vanessa mumbling something under his breath. A smirk crosses the redhead's face and then it looks as if she is trying to hold back laughter. I know she heard what Tripp said. The redhead is carrying a bucket of water, bathing items and a small screen. I know what is coming next and shudder.

Vanessa opens the door to my cell and walks through. The redhead is almost smacked with the swinging cell door that Vanessa released after she walked through. She glares at Vanessa's back. Something makes me think that Vanessa is one nasty piece of work. I look at the redhead who seems to be trying to measure me up.

"She doesn't look like anything special. Are you sure you have the right one for the master?" The redhead looks back at Tripp.

"Oh she's the right one alright." Vanessa responds.

"What makes you so sure?" The redhead responds.

"Because unlike him, I see some of someone from our past in her. She is more than some girl that has latent Fae ability. She is at least half Sidhe, from the otherworld direct." Vanessa informs the redhead.

"Who?" The redhead and Tripp ask in unison.

"You seriously can't see it?" Vanessa looks incredulously at Tripp.

"Obviously not, or I wouldn't be asking." Tripp says in a snotty tone.

"Remember the Sidhe that came to our gathering in San Francisco? The one you killed?" Vanessa retorts.

My mind starts reeling. San Francisco. Tripp was there? My mom! I want to throw up. How could I have been tricked by him, to think he was my friend? He killed my mom!

"Oh that got a response." Vanessa looks back at me. "You know who we are talking about. Don't you?"

"Get away from me." I spit out, the venom dripping from my tone.

"I am not the one who killed her. I saw it happen but I was not the cause." Vanessa shrugs.

"I am confused." Tripp frowns.

So Mr. Confident doesn't know everything. What an asshole! I want to kill him for what he has done to my family.

"Now she knows it is you. You were the one who killed her mom if I am guessing correctly. You're such an idiot." The redhead says smartly.

"Shut up Rachel or I will cut you down where you stand!" Tripp snarls at her.

"Please." Rachel rolls her eyes. "You and what army? You know what abilities we all have but that is all that makes you special. This girl could take you out without any of her abilities, whatever they may be." Rachel retorts.

I quickly look to the water bucket, pulling some water

from it, form it into a spike shape and freeze it. I will it toward Tripp's head. Rachel knocks it out of the air and sends it smashing against the wall. Rachel and Vanessa look at me, seemingly unimpressed.

"Water girl and no fishy look to her. Must be her mother's blood preventing that. No wonder she doesn't look like much. Wonder what other power she has, if any." Rachel looks to Vanessa.

"It doesn't matter, I doubt she will try that again." Vanessa looks at me. "Isn't that right?" Vanessa's dark hair starts changing to have a hint of green to it. Her dark skin lightening slightly with a silvery tint to it. Her fingers now webbed. She is a Merrow!

"Hurry and get her washed up. I will control the water so that she can't use it to attack again." Vanessa commands Rachel, her eyes glowing brightly from the silver ring around her pupil.

Rachel sets down the bucket and the bathing items, then sets up the screen. She turns around and looks at me. Rachel frowns as she glimpses down to the shackle, then smiles as if she just remembered a neat trick.

"Vanessa, can you hold her still a minute? I need to remove some of her clothes. That shackle will cause problems with washing her properly if I don't."

Vanessa pins my arms down at my sides. Rachel grabs my left ankle so that I can't kick her.

"You may want to hold still so that I don't cut you down to the bone. Don't try anything funny or I will." Rachel grins up at me before sticking out her finger.

Rachel's nail begins to grow longer and seems much sharper. She slips her finger under my pant leg and brings it upward. I hear the fabric cutting and tearing as she rises up. Rachel quickly moves and I feel a slight tugging on my left leg and then my jeans are off. I feel slightly embarrassed standing in the room in a shirt and my underwear. I have a feeling I'm about to get even more embarrassed in just a moment as I catch a gleam in Rachel's eyes.

Rachel quickly and delicately slices through the thin satin fabric of my underwear and then up to slice the front of my shirt open. In the process she breaks the snap of my bra and pulls my shirt and bra off my body. I shiver, standing naked with the two girls in my cell. I'm only thankful for the screen that keeps me from being naked in front of anyone else that should happen to come into the room.

I want to cover myself up but with my arms being held tight in place it makes it impossible. Rachel grabs a bath sponge and squirts some gel on it that I'm hoping is soap. She plunges the sponge down into the bucket and then starts to wash down my body. Oh how I wish Vanessa would have warmed up the water before. Goosebumps pop up all over and the cold tightens my skin.

I stand being held in place; wet, cold and shivering. My head is yanked roughly as a towel is being used to dry my hair. Rachel then comes around with another towel and uses it to remove the water from my body; down my arms, chest, stomach and legs. I feel violated.

Rachel then puts the white dress over my head and Vanessa slips my arms into the sleeves. I feel like a live doll being dressed by two girls. Vanessa fastens the back of the dress as Rachel straightens out the skirt. Rachel walks over to the corner of the room and grabs a stool and places it in front of me.

"Sit." She commands.

"I'm not your dog, you could say please." My eyes narrow at her.

Rachel's eyes widen for a quick moment in surprise before she grins back at me. She grabs my arm and pulls me to the stool. She puts her hands on my shoulders and forces me onto the stool

"Morcant will not be pleased if you bruise her, halfwit!" Vanessa snaps at Rachel.

I look back and forth between the two women. If I wasn't in this situation, this thing they have between them might be rather funny. Vanessa comes around behind me and takes my hair in her hands. My hair is twisted and pulled in various directions. I feel like Katniss from the Hunger Games. A sharp metal object scrapes down onto my scalp. I wince.

"There, now she is ready." Vanessa announces. Rachel looks me over and nods in agreement.

"The ceremony will start in a few hours, make sure she doesn't mess anything up." Vanessa informs Tripp.

Tripp nods. He holds out his hand for the keys. Vanessa tosses the keys onto the desk and walks out. Rachel snickers and grabs the door closing it behind her.

CHAPTER 35

Rob

I pace the room back and forth. I thought Nickolai cared for Avalon. Why in the hell would he choose now to run off for alone time? I can't understand what he is thinking. Carl is sparing with Melanie in the yard with Drew watching the two of them. Avalon has been gone for twenty-four hours and the anxiety is torturing me. It is almost evening, we need to be doing something to get her back.

I look back out into the yard. Carl seems to enjoy his new found strength and abilities. I look forward to sharing knowledge with him that I could not share before. It will be nice when we get Avalon back and we can reunite this family. Maybe then I can breathe easier knowing she is safe. The hair on the back of my neck stands up as a chill washes over me. Oh how I wish Nickolai would hurry up!

Nickolai crashes through the trees on the edge of the property and swiftly shifts back to human form while running toward the house. He motions for everyone to go inside. Carl shifts back as well and runs toward the house. Melanie walks over to Drew and picks him up like he is a baby. I guess she is learning to get over the smell or she is just not breathing right now. I chuckle to myself.

"So, do you know where she is? We need to get her now!" I demand, looking directly at Nickolai. Nickolai looks abashed for a moment and then nods

"Carl, do you have a map of Colorado anywhere that I can write on?" Nickolai asks.

"Yes. I have an old Rand McNally map in my study." Carl leaves and promptly returns with the map and lays it out on the kitchen table.

"Based on the knowledge of some of our old safe houses in Colorado, what Avalon said and what I could hear beyond Tripp's annoying voice, she is at the safe house here." Nickolai's finger hits the map just west of a town called Estes Park.

"But that is a tourist town, how could she be hidden there?" Melanie asks.

"He isn't pointing at Estes Park, just west of it. The safe house is not an actual house. It is in some old mines near there." Drew adds.

My head turns in his direction along with everyone else's except for Nickolai.

"Oh right, I forgot to mention that, sorry. I was also part of Morcant's crew. But I was given the choice. When they started doing these mass Awakenings I realized people weren't being given the choice anymore. He was Awakening people without their consent or knowledge. With Nickolai, I found a way to leave too." Drew looks down at the table.

"What's done is done. We will speak of it no more". I look around the room and Drew nods.

"So how do we get to her?" I look at Nickolai and Drew.

"There are two entrances into that safe house. The main entrance and a small service tunnel to the west of it. Luckily the main entrance is easy to find as it is just down the hillside and under the Fall River Visitor Center." Nickolai explains.

"You guys will want to split up." Drew looks at Nickolai.

"Melanie and I will take the service entrance. Carl and Rob, take the main entrance." Nickolai looks around the table.

"Carl, make sure you seem uncertain of yourself, like when you just finished your Awakening. Remember how you felt and use it to your advantage to blend in. Most around you will not be as strong as you are." Nickolai informs Carl.

"Rob, you may need to do something with your glamour magic; you will stand out." Nickolai informs me.

I nod and air shifts around me slightly.

"Yeah that will work, try not to use your abilities much because your eyes light up like Morcant's when he is using his." Nickolai advises.

"Obviously, you will stay here Drew. After this is over,

Avalon will be going with Carl and Rob back to the Sidhe. Melanie and I will return and will figure out our next steps after that." Nickolai looks at Melanie and Drew for their understanding.

"When do we leave?" I look at Nickolai.

"Now."

~*~

Carl parks the Ridgeline in the parking lot of Key Bank. We exit the vehicle stand on the eastside of the vehicle in the shade. The sun is just over the mountain peaks letting me know it is about seven. I just hope Melanie's sunscreen lasts long enough.

"We meet back here at midnight. If one group finds her do not go looking for the other group; just leave with Avalon and come here. If the other group does not come back by midnight, the group with Avalon will leave." Nickolai looks at all of us to make sure we all agree.

"If I do not bring Avalon back with me in the next twenty-four hours someone else will be sent to find her and bring her to the council." I advise.

Nickolai nods. Nickolai heads off toward the main strip of stores with Melanie close behind him. I look at Carl and the anger in his eyes looks like he would burn through everything if he had Superman's powers.

"We will get her back." I tell him as we start following after Nickolai.

"How can you be so sure?" Carl snarls back.

"Because I haven't given up hope. I know in my heart we will be able to reach her in time." I hope with all that I am, that I am right.

A tingling sensation alerts me to someone's presence in my mind.

"You know, just because she is dating Nickolai, that doesn't mean she is married. If you love her like I think you do, you need to fight for her." Carl looks pointedly at me.

I laugh. "Nothing gets pass you, does it?"

Carl nods. *"I'm her dad. I know her, and I feel as if I know you as well."*

I smile. Nickolai looks back at us. I'm sure he is wondering exactly what I am talking about. I nod back at him, acknowledging that I see him.

We walk past the shops that are still open along the strip. The smells from the ice cream and taffy shops fill the air, as a constant breeze blows. My mouth waters involuntarily. I shake my head trying to not let myself be lured in by the sugary sweets. The smell reminds me of the sweets that we once used to lure humans into the Sidhe during Samhain.

We reach the end of the strip and cut back into the trees behind the shops. We stay in the cover of trees skirting the more populated areas so the people do not see how fast we move. Melanie starts swearing. I look at her and her sunscreen has worn off and she is like a ripe tomato.

"We don't have time to reapply, besides the sun has just dipped down behind the mountains. Suck it up and let's go." Nickolai snaps at her.

Melanie glares back at him, her blue eyes glowing brightly. Her skin is already regaining its unusually pale color.

"Nice trick." I tease Melanie making light of her sunburn.

I wink at her trying to lighten the mood. Melanie smiles and nods at me.

With the sun no longer hindering our movements, Carl and Nickolai shift and take off. It is quite the sight to see a black panther and a Siberian tiger running together. Melanie and I take off after them easily keeping up while still sticking close to the trees in case we get too close to the human population.

Running through the trees almost feels like home. No smell of the city, no pollutants, just fresh air. Nickolai and Carl are sitting close to the entrance of an old mine several miles from where we came. Melanie and I approach slowly.

The old mine in front of us is dark and worn down. It does not look like anyone would willingly go in there for fear of collapse. I know from first-hand experience that looks can be deceiving. Nickolai and Melanie go further off to the west to the second entrance. I look at Carl and motion him to lead. Carl sits there looking at me. I feel like a dunce. I wrap the air around me bending it to my will.

Once I am sufficiently cloaked, Carl starts moving off into the mine and I follow close behind. I know he can't see me but I let him know in other ways by touching his back on occasion. I know there was only one that could see me at this point: Morcant who I knew also had fae sight.

We walk through the tunnels looking for any sign of Avalon. There are several tunnels that branch off from this one; some look as if they have been used only by the footprints left in the dirt, and others are blocked off by boards. I stop and look through the boards on one of the blocked off tunnels. Beyond the boards is an old ladder that descends into what I assume is another series of tunnels, but just below the hole in the floor is water burying the ladder in its depths.

"I know you're around here somewhere, let's go." Carl's mind breaks through my own curiosity. I find it curious that he was able to do that when he could not see me. His powers are obviously growing.

As we continue on there is the sound of a large group of people headed in our direction. Carl quickly changes form, only he doesn't quite go back to his normal human form. His eyes glow more silver than gold, his hair all over his body is a dark green, and his skin has a silver shimmer to it. I am impressed. For not knowing what a Merrow looks like he is pretty close, he is just missing the gills and the fins.

People begin filtering into the tunnel and Carl is able to easily blend in with them. The people are all slightly different but their eyes glow either silver, gold or blue. Fae intermingling with Vampires, it is quite a sight. I follow the crowd down the tunnel. A large double door entryway comes up on the left and the crowd starts going through them. I follow the crowd and enter a large cavernous room. It is lit with torch-like sconces all around and in the back of the room is a raised platform. There is a pillar with a metal ring attached to it, like someone could be chained there. Hair stands up on my neck. I need to find Carl.

CHAPTER 36

Nickolai

I walk up to the secondary entrance and motion Melanie to follow. The dark, moisture filled tunnel smells of wet earth and rust. The lack of footprints in this tunnel tells me that no one has used it in a long time, that or no one knows about it. I smile to myself, glad that I thought to scout this place out before I took the job.

Melanie and I continue down the tunnel until it branches off to the left and right. The left tunnel takes us to where new ones are trained before they are allowed to walk free among the population. We take the tunnel to the right. Avalon may be in one of the holding cells in this tunnel. I hope that Tripp is the only one with her when we do find the right cell. The anticipation of ripping him apart makes me smile.

We come to the first door. I slowly open the door as to not make too much noise. It is not the cell I thought it was but a store room. In the middle of the room is a large table with a large binder on it. There are several refrigerator chests lining the walls. This is the blood storage room.

I turn to leave the room when Melanie walks over to the nearest chest and opens it. Her eyes almost bug out of her head at all the blood in it. She looks over at me. I nod at her. Melanie then grabs a bag of blood and downs the entire contents like I used to inhale Red Bull. I chuckle softly to myself. The empty bag is hastily discarded on the floor near the chest.

We leave the room and continue down the tunnel. The next door we come to looks to be made of metal with a lock on it. I try the handle, the door is locked. I smirk. I pull some lock picking tools out of my pocket. Being a juvenile delinquent before the military did have some perks.

I pick the lock and open the door. The room is empty. The cell door is open. There is no light on the table to my left against the wall. A chain hangs from the wall complete with ankle shackles. I look at the dirt floor. This cell has not been used recently.

Just as we are about to leave the room we hear noise in the tunnel outside of it. I pause to listen at the door. There is no one talking but I can hear the feet of possibly two people continuing down the tunnel. The sound of the footsteps sound a bit strange, possibly a shifted fae. I wait for the sound to die down before opening the door. I look down the tunnel and it is empty.

I walk down to the next room, the door is also made of metal with the same type of lock. I try the handle and the door opens. The room is dark, but the smell of melted wax from a candle lingers in the air. The cell door is open.

This cell, unlike the last is made of iron. There is a stool on one side of the cell, the floor is wet on the opposite side. The leg shackles are missing. There is a pile of something on the ground. I bend down to pick it up. It's clothes. I look at them closer. Avalon's pale pink shirt that she was wearing is dirty and torn. I walk over quickly to the candle and touch the wick, it is still warm. It must have been Avalon and Tripp in the tunnel. The odd footsteps were from her ankles being shackled.

I grab Melanie and run out of the room. We run down the tunnel which starts to widen out as it connects to the main tunnel in the safe house. I turn down a narrow tunnel off to the right and pull Melanie behind me. I wince as she scrapes up against the corner of the tunnel opening.

"Sorry, I forgot how sharp that corner is."

"I'm not made of eggshells, I'll survive. Let's just get Avalon and get out of here, the iron cage creeped me out." Melanie shudders.

I walk quickly through the tunnel as it slopes upward. A hole in the wall appears off to the left and I walk toward it. I stop at the hole and find myself looking out what some might consider a balcony to the great room below. I suck in my breath through my teeth at what I see below.

CHAPTER 37

Avalon

Noise from beyond the door tells me the room is full of people. Well, Fae as they call themselves. Being half dragged across the tunnels to this point was annoying. I know what awaits me next and I do not look forward to it, nor do I know how to get out of it. I'm angry that I never got to say goodbye to my family and friends, to tell them that I love them. Now in a matter of an hour or less it won't matter.

My throat tightens and burns, my eyes start to water. I shake my head and will the tears away. I'm determined not to show weakness. I shift slightly on my bare feet, the dirt shuffling beneath them. I smooth out the dress I'm wearing and it feels even more flimsy than the old nightgown I wear that has holes in it. I feel as if anyone looking at me good enough could see right through this thing.

I hear a loud voice boom over the crowd in the room beyond the door. The multitude of voices dims down and only the one voice remains. Whoever he is, his tone and speed in which he talks makes it sound like he is really excited. I already know why. Finally, I will get to meet this person that wants me only for my blood and the life it will give him in exchange.

Tripp looks at me and for a moment I think I see a look of remorse pass his face before it hardens once again in a mask I don't recognize. Tripp leans over and opens the door and ushers me through it.

The room is large and lined with torch-like sconces on the wall. There is a small staircase that leads up onto the raised platform that looks like a stage. On the stage is a tall figure in a dark purple robe. It conceals everything about that person from here; I can't see a face.

Tripp leads me up the stairs and to the robed figure. I don't fight at this point because if I do, all it would take is a good yank and I will fall flat on my ass in front of everyone. Tripp hands my chain to the robed figure and the hand that takes it is a man's, although it is pale white.

I'm unceremoniously yanked further onto the platform and pulled clumsily closer to the robed man. Standing next to him, I look more closely at him. His robe has ornate Celtic knot embroidery along the edges. Around his waist is a thin belt from which a small curved knife hangs.

The man takes my right wrist and grabs ahold of it so hard it hurts and I accidently let a small whimper of pain escape my lips. Tripp unlocks the shackles on my ankles as Morcant holds me tight. I scan the room hoping to find Rob in the crowd just as my visions showed me. My heart sinks as I can't see him anywhere. I spot someone else in the crowd and I feel a hard lump growing in my throat. My dad. What is he doing here?

The man in the robe who I assume is Morcant, throws back his hood revealing what some might call a handsome devil. His dark brown hair is cut short and slicked back on his head. His blue eyes seem even brighter with the silver ring around the pupil. His sharp nose and strong jaw with just a bit of stubble make him seem quite roguish. If he weren't wanting to suck me dry and kill me, I could almost see him as gorgeous. Do all men from the Sidhe look this good?

Morcant looks me over and nods in his approval. Suddenly there is a sharp pain on my finger and just as quickly my finger is in Morcant's mouth. I try to pull away but I can't. Morcant sucks on my finger as he pulls it slowly out of his mouth. He looks to Tripp.

"She is perfect! You have done well."

"Thank you, Master. I only wish to please." Tripp snivels at Morcant's feet.

I snort and roll my eyes to his response.

"Well she doesn't find you so amusing my friend." Morcant looks at me and then at Tripp.

"Total and unbelievable betrayal kills any amusement." I spit out, glaring at Tripp.

"Feisty little thing. I like it. It makes this whole thing even sweeter." Morcant grins down at me.

Come on Dad, Rob, Nickolai, somebody! I know what is going to happen next; if you are planning a rescue now is the time! There is a slight glow that comes from the left out of the corner of my eye. I quickly look to where the light is brighter for a moment and there he is. Rob, he does not shine as much as he did in my visions but I'm beginning to think those are exaggerated.

The look in Rob's eyes do not look like they did in my visions. Now, they have a scared and worried look in them. I wonder what has changed to make his expression seem so grim. My pulse starts to speed up as my anxiety level increases.

CHAPTER 38

Rob

I step back in shock as I see Avalon being brought up on the platform. She is a vision in the white dress she is wearing, even with the scowl on her face that shows she is not going so willingly. I knew this was coming even though we had tried to avoid it. It was also who brought her onto the platform that had me staring in disbelief. I blink several times hoping that the next time I open them that I do not see him bringing her to Morcant. It doesn't work. I would never have guessed that Morcant recruited our changelings too.

My heart sinks into my stomach. This just got a hundred times worse. I scan the room and notice a few others that I recognized from the Sidhe, others that had gone into the changeling program.

"Shit!" I keep my voice down but Carl and some around me look in my direction. I wave them off but I notice Carl looking at me with a worried expression on his face.

"*What is it?*" Carl's voice asks in my head.

"*There are changelings here as well as Awakened.*"

"*And that's bad? Will that keep us from saving her?*"

"*Yes, it's bad. Although they are not as strong as Nickolai, you or myself, they are stronger than these newly Awakened. Two of them I knew from my childhood but they never went through the ceremony to bring their abilities to their fullest potential. The problem in the mortal realm is bigger than I or the council realized.*"

"*Problem?*" Carl's voice rises slightly in pitch.

"*If Morcant is also recruiting changelings that do not have any knowledge of their former lives and then Awakens them, they are stronger and pose more of a threat than the others.*"

"*I'll ask again, will that cause a problem for you with saving her, if it comes between saving her and killing them?*"

I sigh. "*No, it won't be a problem for me. Avalon is more important. The changelings would agree with me if they knew who they really are.*"

I see Carl thinking hard about something, his mind closed off. I prod back into his mind.

"*Care to share?*"

"*With the new problem thrown into the mix, I know what must be done. The ultimate goal is to get Avalon to safety, you got that? Nothing else matters, nothing.*"

"*I understand that, but the tone you are using is worrying me.*"

"*Nickolai and Melanie can cause a distraction as they move from the back to the front of this room. You will get my daughter out of here and to the Sidhe. Morcant is mine!"*

"NO! You don't stand a chance against Morcant!"

Carl shakes his head. *"Believe me, I have thought this through. Nickolai will make a bee line to Avalon killing anyone in his path. You and I both know he is not strong enough to take on Morcant. You made it possible and now I am stronger than him. Melanie could really give two shits about my daughter. You on the other hand love her and I know you will do what is best for her. If you were to go against Morcant and not win this, the rest of us have no clue on how to get Avalon to the Sidhe, and we won't be able to wait around for the council to send someone else. It has to be me. If the worst happens, call Scott. He will take you where you need to go."*

I think over what he says and it seems sound. I wonder why he wants me to call his pilot. Why would we need the plane? I nod my head at Carl, deferring to his judgment.

"I will let the others know of the plan, just not all of it." I look up to where Nickolai and Melanie are stationed in the balcony at the back of the room.

"Nickolai, I need you and Melanie to charge up the back. Feel free to kill anyone that stands in your way. If you make it to Avalon before I do, get her out of here. Carl and I will separate her from Morcant."

I finish telling Nickolai the plan in general and the only thing I get from him is a deep growl and he is looking toward the platform. I glance back and Avalon is dangerously close to Morcant. The look on her face is one of utter revulsion mixed with fear. I look back at Nickolai and see him jump off the balcony and phases mid-air and lands in the crowd with

Melanie on his heels.

"Now or Never!" I yell at Carl over the crowd that is now starting to get louder with Nickolai and Melanie tearing through them.

I start running through the crowd as their attention is drawn to the back of the room. I feel large icicles whiz by my head heading for Morcant. Carl sure isn't wasting time. I look back at him with my eyes wide.

"Sorry, slipped in the aim a bit there."

"Yeah sure, just concentrate."

I watch as the first icicle plunges into Morcant's side and he releases a loud cry, his mouth drips with blood as he pulls away from Avalon's throat. He turns in Carl's direction and reflects the rest. I look at Avalon hoping we were able to distract him soon enough. She is breathing but is slightly paler than before.

I pull out the daggers I have hidden behind my back and start slicing my way through the crowd as I pass. There is one left as I get to the platform and as she turns, I recognize her. Audrina. She grins at me as she flashes her own set of daggers at me. She doesn't have a spark of recognition on her face as she looks at me, she just knows I do not belong here. I steel myself for what I know I must do, knowing that when I get home I will have to face her parents when I tell them she is dead.

We circle each other. I try hard to focus on the girl before me and look for an opening. She lunges forward and I spin just outside of her reach and then bring my daggers in and slice into the extended arm and across her ribs. She screams in pain and anger as she twists around. The blood flows freely from her arm which is now hanging limply at her side. I notice the slice across her ribs went deeper than I anticipated and caught a lung. This will end faster than I thought. We circled again and she makes another desperate lunge. I step back as she falls. She is trying to breath but I know the blood now in her lung is making that hard. I feel pity for her.

"I'm sorry Audrina." I whisper in her ear as I slice her throat open from ear to ear.

I get up to the platform and sheath my daggers. I notice that Morcant seems to be toying with Carl and his icicles of various sizes.

It seems Carl was only able to get that one hit in. Morcant is bleeding from the wound caused by the icicle in his right side. The wound is just low enough that it did not hit anything vital. His wound will heal within a day if he survives. I look at Carl and can see the knicks his own reflected icicles has caused him.

I run over to Avalon and lift her up gently, looking around for the best exit. I glare at the man that brought Avalon to the platform as he sneaks out the back door, too cowardly to join in battle. I would love to be able to put Avalon down and chase after him, but I will take care of him later, there is nowhere he can run where I will not be able to find him.

I look down at Avalon's face and her beauty takes my breath away. I quickly work to heal the wound on her neck to prevent more blood loss. A full healing will have to wait until we are away from here. I wipe the tears from her face.

"We will be out of here soon, everything will be

alright." I whisper to her.

Avalon nods. "I knew you would save me." Avalon says weakly as she smiles up at me. I just want to wrap her up in my arms and never let go. To whisk her off to the Sidhe and never let anything more happen to her, but I can't.

"Rob!"

I turn toward the voice yelling my name, and see a knife coming straight for my head.

CHAPTER 39

Melanie

I follow behind Nickolai into the swarm of people below. They don't even know what hit them as they crumple to the ground. Although Nickolai truly stinks, the power that he wields and that seems to also radiate off of him is alluring. I push my lustful thoughts to the back of my mind. Now is not the time. I admonish myself.

I jump from body to body as they start to pile up in Nickolai's wake and finish them off by nails, hands or teeth. It feels good to not feel weak, to feel this powerful, and useful at the same time. I take a glance at the front of the room and notice it isn't Rob that is fighting Morcant but Carl! This was not the plan that I remembered.

As we reach the front of the crowd a man turns and throws his knife at Rob and Avalon. I yell out to Rob, but I doubt he has time to avoid it. I spurn myself forward willing myself to go faster than I ever have before. I jump off the man that threw the knife, thrusting him toward Nickolai. I panic as I don't think I will be able to make it before it hits them. I do the only thing I can think of and take off my shoe and throw it. I watch as it hits the knife and it sails past Rob's face, nicking his ear in the process, and clatters against the rock wall.

I hear a guttural roar and look toward the noise. Carl phases into a large black panther as he lunges for Morcant, his claws extended and maw open wide. It is a sight to behold as the icicles Carl was throwing continue their assault on Morcant. The shift to the panther seems to have caught Morcant off guard as three ice daggers pierce into him and he cries out angrily.

The gleam in Morcant's eyes seem to brighten as he realizes what Carl is. It is then that I realize what Carl's plan is. A fight to the death, the death being his. We all know Carl is not strong enough to take on Morcant alone. I don't say anything. I know Carl is on a suicide mission at this point. I don't want to distract him and get him killed. He is giving us a chance to get out safely.

Rob carries Avalon towards Nickolai and me. It feels like everyone else in the room is standing here entranced by the fight taking place on the platform. Avalon starts to struggle in Rob's arms, so he puts her down but does not let her go. He keeps an arm around her to keep her steady. She looks at her father and Morcant in disbelief.

Loud snarling and growling fill the room as Carl continues to shred clothing and skin off of Morcant. Carl's fur is matted in blood as there are several gashes in his sides as well as the blood flows from his wounds. Carl lunges several times with his jaws snapping, trying fervently to reach Morcant's throat.

The ice daggers are still flying but it is not aimed for anyone in particular, just in a general direction, toward the two grappled in a match to the death. It seems as though there is control by more than one person. I look at Avalon, wondering if it is her, but the look on her face tells me she is not controlling anything, it is plastered in panic. I look back at Carl and Morcant and distinctly hear the piercing of flesh as one of the ice daggers strikes home.

A sharp animal cry resounds and I see that the dagger has gone into the ribs of Carl. Carl starts to slow and his accuracy fails as he swipes at air.

"This is not going to end well. We need to get out of here now!" I yell at the others.

"No, I will not leave my dad! If you want to leave and save yourself go for it. I would expect nothing less from you, Melanie!" Avalon spits at me in anger, her eyes dangerously bright.

I look back to the fight, backing up towards the entrance. Morcant stabs Carl on the other side puncturing the other lung. With the inability to breathe Carl slumps forward. Morcant rolls with Carl and pins him down to the floor. Morcant opens his mouth wide and plunges his teeth down into the flesh of Carl's exposed neck.

A scream of agony and anger fills the room followed by the sound of rushing water, a lot of water. Walls of water burst into the room from every opening, pounding into anything in its path before sweeping it up in its swirling depths. I look at the others and they were desperately trying to get Avalon out but there was nowhere to go. I run to the group.

"Avalon, in order for us to get out you need to control the water around us to keep us alive! I don't have to breathe, but you will kill Rob and Nickolai if you don't do what I'm asking."

The look on her face is a mask of rage, I have no idea if what I said made it through to her, through her rage of anger and despair. The water is up to our waists, pulling at our bodies forcefully. I look toward Morcant and watch as wave after wave pummels into him, some he is able to deflect, but soon the waves overwhelm him. The water is red with blood, making my mouth water profusely. I steel myself against the tempting urge to drink some of it. I know it is not the blood I need, it is the blood of Fae and Were, which for me is tainted. My fear of becoming something like Morcant helps me fight my urges.

Suddenly the water recedes from us but sweeps through the room going up and over our heads. Bodies swirl around in the water, being slammed into other bodies and objects. It feels like we are stuck in a waterproof bubble as we rise up from the floor and move slowly out of the room with the rushing water. I look at Avalon and her eyes are full of silver light, I can see no other color and the look on her face chills me to the core. There is no emotion on it. It is like she is staring at nothing.

The bubble exits the tunnels and deposits us on the side of the hill. The water recedes from us and we watch it rush down to meet the river. The sky looks like it opened up and is pouring water. I watch in horror as the waters continue to rise in the river, its banks overflowing as it heads toward Estes Park.

"Avalon! You have to stop. If you don't stop you are going to kill a lot of innocent people! The water you have unleashed is going to flood towns!"

A sob breaks out from Avalon and the light dims. The rain continues but not as heavy. The water recedes from the tunnels. I look to the river which appears about five feet higher than normal. The damage is done, there is no way to stop this now. I look back to Avalon and Nickolai is now carrying her still form in his arms. She looks so small and harmless. It is hard to imagine that she could have produced such destruction.

"Follow me, we will head out to Granby. Carl's car is about to be filled with water if it isn't already." Nickolai mutters quietly.

As we follow Nickolai through the woods up to the main road the events of the day seem to take its toll on all of us. Rob's head hangs low in defeat, I know he feels the loss of Carl. Even though he wasn't Carl's son, I am sure the two of them were quite close. Nickolai seems focused even more on Avalon, as if he is the only one that can protect her. I think back to what I have witnessed before and wonder if he has seen the connection that I have between Avalon and Rob.

Even though I didn't know Carl very well, and I know I treated Avalon like crap over the last several months, I still feel bad about her losing her dad too. Ok, ever since I met her, I've treated her like crap. I feel like the biggest ass ever to walk the planet. I trudge behind the others as we come up on the first motel we see as we enter Granby.

CHAPTER 40

Rob

I follow Nickolai up to the Homestead Motel. I take Avalon from him, cradling her in my arms gently. She seems so fragile, so much smaller than the larger than life being she was earlier. It makes me wonder what exactly we saw. If that is a glimpse at the girl of the prophesy, it was a scary yet glorious sight to behold. Nickolai goes into the office to secure our room.

"Melanie, it will be light soon. Make your way back to the tunnels to hide out in until sunset. Then go back to Drew. We will speak with you again soon and plan our next steps. If you run into others like yourself and Drew that want to join our cause, use Carl's home as your safe house." I tell her.

Melanie looks at me and I can tell she is not sure if she should take direction from me or wait for Nickolai to come back and tell her. I sigh.

"Avalon will want the house used for this purpose, I

can assure you. Since no one knows about it you and Drew and any others you might find will be safe there as long as you follow the rules Nickolai gave you before. While you are in the tunnels, go to the storage rooms and fill some of the bags in there with the blood bags in the freezers."

Nickolai walks out of the motel office with keys in hand and looks at Melanie. Nickolai throws his phone to her.

"Here, call Drew and let him know you're coming home. I will be continuing on with Avalon and Rob." Nickolai looks at me and I know that trying to talk him out of coming is not going to work.

Melanie pockets Nickolai's phone and nods before running off in the direction we came. Nickolai turns and I follow him. We walk past four rooms before stopping at the room on the bottom level at the end of the building. Nickolai opens the door and walks through, holding it open so that I can bring Avalon into the room easier.

The room is dark and cool. There are two double beds with multicolored, blue floral comforters on them. There is a small desk with a chair next to the television in front of the beds. Next to the window is a table with two chairs. At the far end is a sink and another doorway to the bathroom.

Nickolai walks over to the nearest bed and pulls down the covers and then moves so that I can lay Avalon in the bed. I put Avalon in the bed and pull the covers over her to tuck her in. She shivers slightly then whimpers in her sleep. I want to pick her back up and hold her securely to my body.

There is a movement and I look up to see Nickolai slip into the other side of the bed, thankfully with his clothes on, but it still does not ease the beast of jealousy that wants to tear out of me and fling him across the room. I ignore my jealousy and stand up looking at Nickolai.

"Don't try anything!"

"Oh like I would. I won't take advantage of her while she is unconscious. She is freezing and she will warm up and be more comfortable with a body near her."

I tighten my jaw at his retort of her being unconscious. I walk over to the desk and settle into the chair watching Nickolai lay his head down on the pillow and holding Avalon close to his body. Within moments, Nickolai's snoring fills the room. I laugh to myself, and wonder how Avalon could sleep through the noise in her ear.

I sit back in the chair and pull out the necklace that has been against my skin hidden from view ever since I got back from the Sidhe. Trieva's necklace. I try to think about the best way to tell Avalon the rest of the truth that she needs to know before we reach the Sidhe. I worry that once she knows what I still have to tell her she will not want to continue further. I put the necklace into my pocket. I will be giving it to its new owner soon.

I quietly pick up the phone and make a call to Carl's pilot, Scott. The phone rings several times before a frantic man answers on the other end.

"Hello?"

"Scott, this is Rion. I need you to bring my father's plane to the Granby airport now. It needs to be fueled and ready to leave in three hours."

"Do you have any idea what is going on around here? Everywhere is on alert for flooding. Estes Park is half under water, Lyons is an island! It's more than just the Poudre River that is flooded!"

"Look, I know about the flooding alright! I need the plane out here now. I can't get the family out of here without it!" I look at the two sleeping people on the bed, glad that my yelling into the phone did not wake them.

Scott sighs. "Alright. I'll be out there as soon as I can. I'll head to the airport now."

I hang up the phone without saying goodbye. I pull out my phone from my pocket and look at the map that I had saved earlier. The nearest intersection of ley lines is near Salt Lake City, Utah. It wasn't my usual entry point but it will have to do. I can still call the gateway from there. I get up from the chair and sit in the floor and move into position for meditation. I can sleep when I get home.

I hear someone stirring and it pulls me out of my meditative state. I open my eyes and see that both Avalon and Nickolai are waking up. I glance at my phone. Two more hours until the plane will be ready to leave.

"We need to be ready to leave in an hour, get showered and dressed so we can go." I announce.

Avalon slowly gets up, and makes her way gingerly to the bathroom, as if her body is sore all over. Nickolai starts to follow her. I get up quickly and grab his arm before he makes it pass me to the bathroom.

"Not so fast. We need to talk and set some ground rules that you must follow when we enter the Sidhe." I look at him firmly.

"Couldn't you tell us both at the same time?" Nickolai looks at me in annoyance.

"I would think you would like to know what you are getting yourself into if you plan on continuing a relationship with her," I say with a smirk as his eyebrow raises.

"First and foremost," I continue, "Avalon will not need added stress during this time, but I can't forbid her to see you. You need to keep things slow with her until this plays itself out."

Nickolai's eyes narrow at me, not liking what I have to say to him. I admit I am getting a little satisfaction out of this, as some of it is true and some not so much but it works better for me. I continue on before he can say anything.

"Before we head out to the airport, we need to grab you some food and water. This is important. The food we get here is the only food that you can eat and the only thing you can drink. When we enter the Sidhe, you must not eat or drink anything offered to you. That is rule one."

"What about Avalon?" Nickolai asks.

"Avalon is Sidhe, these rules do not apply to her," I reply curtly.

"Second, if you start hearing music, plug your ears right away. Not all music in the Sidhe has malicious effects but just to be safe." I hand him a pair of industrial ear plugs.

"Never ask personal or direct questions of anyone you meet. It is considered rude and the Sidhe will always punish you for it. Never show weakness. It can and will be exploited. This is another reason I would advise against going too fast with Avalon and letting it show. No PDA, got it? Otherwise you will be used as each other's weakness."

Nickolai nods. I look at him and he seems to be handling this well so far. I chuckle inwardly. If he follows all of these or not, he will make it easier for me to spend time with Avalon.

"Do not lie. We can tell when you are lying. Always be polite. Your sarcasm will do you no favors. Never, and I mean never, say thank you when receiving anything."

"How is saying thank you bad?" Nickolai asks in disbelief.

"I know it is confusing since that is a polite thing to say here. In the Sidhe it is considered rude and will deeply offend whoever you say it to. If you want to thank them, offer them a gift instead of saying the words. Remember that the value of the gift is not important, it is the act of giving that is important."

"Wow, do you have all this written down? All the rules will be hard to remember." Nickolai sighs in exasperation.

"No. Those are just general rules of etiquette that you must follow and master. Ignorance of the rules is not tolerated and second chances are rarely given," I state sharply.

Nickolai nods. The bathroom door opens and Avalon steps out, her dark hair dripping wet, wearing the stained white dress from last night. I wish she could be presented in better fashion but we have no time to get new clothes that would not look ridiculous. Nickolai walks over to Avalon, hugs her close and kisses her on the forehead before walking into the bathroom.

"Avalon come sit with me." I walk to the nearest bed and sit down patting the spot next to me. "There are a few things we need to talk about before we leave."

Avalon walks toward me and sits down next to me on the bed. I turn to face her before I speak again.

"There is more I need to tell you before you go to join your mother's family in the Sidhe." I reach into my pocket and pull out Trieva's necklace and then hand it to Avalon.

"This was your mother's, now it belongs to you. This represents not only your heritage, but your family line. This necklace is worn by the heir to the High Throne of the Sidhe." I stop and look up at her as I watch my words sink in. Avalon's mouth drops in shock. I smile reassuringly at her.

"You will be fine, but there are some rules of etiquette that you must follow while you are in the Sidhe. There will be other rules to follow once we reach the palace. The rules you need to know now will aid in your acceptance from the people once you are pronounced as heir." I state in a serious tone.

"Wait! Stop, rewind and freeze!" She blurts out.

I chuckle inwardly as she quotes Princess Diaries. "What?" I manage to get out with a straight face.

"You mean I have no choice in this? It's just how it is and I have to accept it?" Her voice gets shriller as panic starts to creep in.

"You will always be who you are. You will get to

choose whether or not to pass the obligation to your child if you have any. You reached the age of decision on your birthday in June. You must learn what it is to be Sidhe; our culture and rules. You need to know before you can decide whether to accept it or reject it."

Avalon seems to calm slightly at this.

"So these rules that you will need to follow are quite different than what you are used to. The Sidhe, as you will learn, are not like humans. You must always be polite."

Avalon snorts at that.

"I mean it! Even if you don't mean it you must always say things politely, even when delivering bad news to someone, say it in a polite way. Until you get to the Palace, do not ask direct or personal questions to those you meet as it is considered rude. This rule of course does not apply to the High King, Queen, and heir."

"So you're saying until I am announced as Heir I shouldn't act as if I am the Heir?"

"Exactly. For your safety, I want to keep your true identity a secret. Never show weakness. There are those that if they know your weakness, will exploit it and use it against you. It is because of this that I warn you not to be overly obvious about your feelings for any male while you are in the Sidhe. Only if you are prepared to marry him are you let anyone know. Marriage will make you stronger, especially if you are married to the one that was destined for you.

"But how will I know who is destined for me to marry? Why do I have to marry at all?"

"You don't have to marry but I am sure at some point in your life you will want to. As for who you are destined to marry, I am sure you will find that out for yourself when the time is right."

"You know all this being thrust on me totally sucks. Just so you know." She folds her arms across her chest.

I ignore the incredibly sexy pout on her face and continue on.

"Do not lie. The people of the Sidhe can tell when you are lying. Oh and unless you want to piss the Sidhe off, never say thank you to them after receiving a gift. It is offensive. If you want to thank them, give them a gift in return. It doesn't matter the value, just the act of giving that the Sidhe appreciate."

"Have you told Nickolai all this too? This is quite a load of shit to remember, Rob!"

"I have. There are additional rules he has to follow because he isn't of the Sidhe. He won't be able to eat or drink anything there as well."

"So he can't stay there for long, can he?"

"No, not unless you want him to stay there forever. The food and drink will also cause him to forget everything. If you want to keep him safe, you need to help him follow those rules."

Avalon nods as she puts on her necklace.

"Until we are at the palace, wear that under your dress. There are those of the Unseelie Court that would love to get their hands on that by any means necessary."

"Unseelie Court?"

"That is more information than you need to know at this point. You are tired, weak and I have given you more than enough to think about. When we get you home, I promise to tell you all you will ever need to know, okay?"

"I'll hold you to that." She looks at me seriously.

"Of that, I have no doubt, my princess." I bow my head slightly.

The bathroom door opens and Nickolai walks into the room toweling off his hair. He glances at Avalon.

"I take it that he read the riot act to you too?" Nickolai asks.

"Yep," Avalon replies, accentuating the p.

CHAPTER 41

Avalon

Nickolai stands just outside the bathroom toweling his hair dry. I try not to drool in front of Rob since he is sitting right next to me. Nickolai is only wearing jeans, his shoes and socks still in the bathroom with his shirt. I watch every muscle move on his chiseled body. His tanned skin shows off his muscles to perfection. I look from his chest to his perfectly toned eight pack. A light trail of dark hair runs from his belly button down below the waistband of his jeans. A tease to see what's under there.

Rob clears his throat, breaking me out of my day dreaming. I do a quick mental check; no drool, mouth is not hanging open, no heavy breathing. I start to relax. Nickolai goes back into the bathroom to hang up the towel and grabs the rest of his things.

We leave the motel and return the keys to the front desk. Rob then leads us to the nearest convenience store where he promptly starts filling the bag with water and protein bars. As Nickolai grabs a few Mt. Dew, Rob waves him off.

"No Pop. It will not help you where we are going." Rob takes the bag to the register and pays for the items in it before walking out of the store. I quickly follow him with Nickolai right behind me. We continue walking through Granby until we reach the small airport. As we get out to the strip I see my dad's plane waiting for us.

"Where are we going?" I ask Rob.

"Salt Lake City, but that isn't our final stop, we will have further to go before we reach the gateway." Rob replies.

We enter the plane and I take a seat next to one of the tables. I kick off my shoes to feel the plush beige carpet on my feet. Nickolai sits in front of me on the other side of the table. Rob continues to the cockpit to give Scott his instructions.

"So this is the type of life you are used to?" Nickolai looks around in amazement.

"Yes and no. My dad came from a well off family and inherited most of his wealth, including this plane. It allowed my dad to pursue his artistic interests. Those paintings in the front room are all his," I say.

"Why did you even bother to work?" Nickolai asks.

"I needed something to do with my life, not have everything handed to me." I say sharply. I want to take the bite out of my words. He didn't deserve to get his head bitten off at an honest question, but I can't.

"I don't want to talk about the way my life used to be. I

need to think, I'm sorry." I get up and walk back to one of the individual seats in the back of the plane. Nickolai does not follow but watches me as I sit down. I turn and look out the window. The plane starts to move and I watch as we move down the runway.

I sit back and close my eyes as the plane lifts off the ground. Not because I am afraid of flying, I'm not. I am afraid of looking anyone in the eye right now and losing it. I hate crying in front of others. And the pain of not having my dad with me now is very hard to deal with. I just want to sleep and wake up to this all being a very elaborate, creeptastic dream.

CHAPTER 42

Melanie

To be honest, I feel like I am being left out of everything. Maybe it's just jealousy rearing its ugly head again. The others get to go to a fabulous other land and I get stuck here, with a crippled Drew and try to find others that might join our cause. Maybe this will put all that time in speech class (that I thought was a sheer waste of time,) to good use. I head back toward the tunnels to escape the daylight that is fast approaching. I can feel my body getting sluggish. I make it back into the wet tunnels and into the nearest store room before everything goes dark.

I wake up and it takes me a moment to remember where I am. I get up off the ground where I unceremoniously must have done a face plant earlier. I really need to work on that. I grab a bag hanging from a rack on the wall, and start filling it with blood bags from the freezer. With two full bags I leave the storage room. Just as I am about to take off, I hear a faint sobbing.

Whoever is still here was not with Morcant, or they would have left with him. I seriously doubt Avalon's flood killed him. I follow the sound through the tunnels, hoping that when I find the source of the crying I'm not also hopelessly lost. I finally come to a large cavern higher up in the tunnels, the ground still dry. The room is filled will cages, and all of them are full!

I walk through the room and each cage holds a new Vampire just like me, but not. The last cage I come to, I recognize its occupant.

"Brittany! Are you ok? Why are you all in cages?"

"We were told this is how we would remain until we could control ourselves and not bite and tear at everything. We are all hungry and haven't seen anyone in quite a while. Please help us, the hunger burns!" Brittany cries harder.

I know the burn all too well. I feel it myself but not as strongly as I used to when Nickolai told me how to cope with it. I look around me. There are twenty-five cages in this room. How in the hell am I going to train them, when I just barely had control myself?

I thought back to what Nickolai taught me. First, I needed to get their hunger under control or they would not listen to what I had to say to them. I went back to the front of the room and grab five blood bags out of the bags that I had dropped outside of the entrance. I came back into the room and some of them start throwing themselves against their cages.

"You need to calm down if you want to receive anything. Those that don't, you can rot in your cage for all I care!" My voice booms over the noise and echoes off the walls. The ones throwing themselves against their bars stop.

"Hold out your hands and you will all receive what you crave. It will be just enough to curb the burn so that we can have a chat." I opened the first blood bag, resisting the urge to tear into it and drink it all. I start dripping small portions of blood into the waiting hands. Each bag I open is harder to resist than the last. By the time I finish distributing the blood, my own hunger is burning inside me. I take what little is left and pour it into my hand showing them that I take less than them, showing my control. It isn't enough but it will need to be for now and I steel myself against the burn.

"Before I can let you out of the cages you will need to prove you can control yourself and will not become a killing machine every time you smell blood or are near a human. I know what you are thinking because I have had the same thoughts over the past few days. I had help which obviously you have not. That changes today if you accept my offer." I call out to those in the cages.

"I offer you the chance of vengeance against those who are with Morcant, and ultimately Morcant himself who made us into what we are today. We are no longer human and it will take time before we can blend in with them without being noticed as different. I promise to help you with this and together we will learn all we can about what we can do.

"Do you mean to keep us in these cages inside this dark cave?" A male voice calls out.

"You will be released from the cages if you can prove you can control yourself and you agree to join us." I call out to him.

"Who is us?" Another voice calls out.

"I have joined others more powerful than any of us, who also desire to see Morcant dead. Not just for what he has done to us, but will do to others, possibly even our family and friends until he rules this world. If you want to live under his rule, that is fine. I will leave you here to do so."

"Where are these friends of yours? I do not see anyone else." A woman's voice calls out from the back.

"My friends have gone to their realm to speak with their King to seek his assistance in taking down Morcant. They will be able to take away Morcant's power with the aid from the King." I was making this stuff up as I went because I had no idea what would come of their travels to the Sidhe, but I had to make it sound good for them and myself.

"If you want the chance I offer; the chance for vengeance, for justice, and eventually some normalcy, tell me now."

Every last cage rattles as their occupants all resound in agreement to join our cause. I smile.

"Well we will start with our control then. Once you can open a bag like I did and not take any of the blood within it, I will let you out. When we are all out, I will take you home, where we can all learn from each other."

It is time for the real work to begin.

CHAPTER 43

Avalon

"Avalon."

I'm being gently shaken awake by someone. The voice seems familiar.

"Avalon, baby, wake up please."

A hand brushes my hair out of my face. My eyes flutter open, and I recognize who is in front of me. My eyes narrow. If it wasn't for him, my world would not be so completely upside down. If it wasn't for him, my dad would still be alive.

"Go away. I don't want to see you right now. If you never came to Colorado, my dad would still be alive."

I see the hurt cross Nickolai's face. I know it is not all his fault but right now I need someone to blame, and he is the closest person I can lay any blame on. I turn and face the window fighting against the tears that are threatening to spill over. I close my eyes and wait. I hear Nickolai walk toward the front of the plane.

I look out of the window. The plane is still and the stairs are already in position for us to disembark. The sun is shining brightly but I wish it was cloudy and rainy to match my mood. Can't I just hide in a cocoon so nothing can ever hurt again?

"Avalon, we need to get going. Can you meet us outside in a few minutes, or do you want me to wait for you here?"

Just like Rion, Rob seems to know exactly what I need.

"No. I will be out in a moment." I mutter quietly.

"Ok, I will wait for you at the bottom of the stairs." Rob walks to the front of the plane.

I wait until I can see him leave before I bother to stand up. I walk to the lavatory in the back of the plane to have a private moment. I close the door behind me before I crumple onto the toilet seat and cry my eyes out.

I am not sure how much time has passed before there are no more tears that come, but I know I can't breathe through my nose any more. My breath hitches and I know that if anyone asks me a question when I get outside I will not be able to talk for fear that I will lose it again. I move over to the sink and splash some cold water on my face before drying it with a paper towel.

I look in the mirror, my eyes are red from crying. Nothing to help that. I steel myself against my pain and open the lavatory door. Just as I am about to pass my seat I see a pair of dark sunglasses on it. I smile and then realize whoever set these on the seat heard me lose it. My jaw clenches as I put the glasses on and walk out of the plane and down the stairs to join the others.

A dark sedan pulls up in front of us and the driver gets out. The man walks around and opens the door for me to enter the car. I look to Rob who nods. I duck into the car and Rob gets in on the other side, while Nickolai rides shotgun. He hasn't said a word, and I feel bad that I snapped at him. I'm still not ready to apologize for it though.

The car pulls out and takes us out of the Salt Lake City Municipal Airport and onto the interstate. I lay my head back and close my eyes, my glasses still on my face. No one says anything and right now I am glad of it.

"Avalon, it's time to go." Rob whispers to me as he squeezes my hand.

I open my eyes. Shit, I fell asleep! I just hope that I did not snore while I was passed out in the car with my head tilted back like that. I look around but no one is staring at me funny but everyone is getting out of the car except for the driver. I move to open my door but it is opened from the outside. Rob bends down and grins at me before extending his hand. I take his offered hand and he assists me out of the car. How did I not notice the dimples?

"We are almost home." Rob sighs in relief.

Home. I am not sure what that means anymore. Home used to be where my parents were, then where my dad was. I never considered my apartment home, not really. I nod absently. I just want to feel numb for now.

The car drives off breaking me out of my thoughts. I look around and see that we are standing in front of a campground for Mirror Lake. It must be somewhere in Utah. I couldn't have been asleep that long. I look around and it feels like it's a bit late in the afternoon based on how high the sun is.

Rob takes the lead and I follow, with Nickolai slinging his backpack over his shoulder and following behind me. We walk pass the campground and around the lake edge. I look around and there is no one else around, it is just the three of us.

"Rob, where are we going?" I call out to him.

Rob turns around but continues to walk. I am ready for him to trip and fall over since he isn't watching where he is going, but he doesn't.

"The nearest intersection of ley lines is just up ahead. The power is stronger there and the gateway can be opened easier from there."

"Oh." I don't know what else to say to that since I have no clue what he is talking about.

I look back at Nickolai to see if he knows what Rob is talking about. He looks back at me and shrugs as if he hasn't got a clue either. Morcant must not have clued him into that little detail. I smile smugly.

We reach a small stretch of land that juts out into the lake. Trees surround the area and almost do not clear until the water's edge. There is a log near the edge of the water that looks well worn. I look around and Nickolai has set his pack down and is stretching, while Rob seems to be looking for something.

I walk over to Rob. "What exactly are you looking for?" I ask him curiously.

"I'm not anymore, I have found it. I just need time to prepare." He looks to where several trees have bent together forming a natural archway just in front of the water's edge.

"How long will it take?" I secretly hope it's not within the next few minutes.

"About an hour. I need to be fully focused in order to light the rune," Rob explains.

"The rune?" I ask in confusion.

"In between the trees that make the arch. Do you see the flat stone beneath the arch?"

I look over to the arch way and down to the ground underneath it. Why didn't I see that stone before? It was flat with a variety of colors on it. In the center of the stone I could see that something was carved into it.

I walk over to the stone and look down. The carving in the stone looks like something out of my old, world mythology book.

"What does this rune mean?" I ask Rob as I point at it.

"It is our symbol for gateway," Rob replies.

Is it really as easy as he makes it seem? I watch as Rob sets his things down and sits with his legs crossed in front of the stone. I leave him to his meditation and walk over to the log and sit down. I look out over the water. The water is so clear I can see the rocks at the bottom and a few lake trout swimming around them.

I take out the necklace Rob gave me in the hotel room. It looks different than I remember it. I run my fingers over the gold trinity knot in the center of it before moving along the outer silver ring encasing it. The dragon on the necklace grasps the circle with its claws, its body covered by the knot. It's my favorite part. The dragon's body is made of gold and silver with four limbs, a tail and wings that are only half open. The dragon. It didn't used to look like this. It used to hug the knot and circle. Now it looks like it is alert and watching me.

I let out a sigh. Everything seems to be going a thousand miles a minute. Every time I have turned something new happens and throws me for a loop. First I was a freak, now I'm a royal freak. I blow away some of my hair that has fallen in my face. So much has happened and I don't even know which way is up. I wonder if this is how Rion felt when he was taken to the Sidhe after Mom died.

My anger rises with the thought of my mom's death and then my dad's. Tripp, I would see him destroyed for what he did to my family. My jaw clenches tight almost to the point of being painful. My hands clench into fists and I can feel my nails go into my palms. No longer. No longer will I allow anyone to fight in my stead. This is my fight. I will learn all that I can and I will put an end to this.

I can hear Rob muttering something but it doesn't sound like he is speaking English. I can't make out what he is saying. I get up from the log and stiffly walk over to where Rob is standing. I can feel a difference in the air.

Nickolai walks up behind me. "I will make this right Avalon. I promise you."

I look up at Nickolai and see the sincerity on his face.

"I know you will. Look, I'm sorry about lashing out at you like that earlier. I think I just needed someone to blame."

"I understand. Are we good?" He asks hopefully.

"We are getting there." I smile at him.

I look back at Rob and there is a shimmering silver gateway in front of him. The rune in the stone glows a brilliant blue.

"Whoa!" Nickolai and I say at the same time.

Rob grins back at me. "You haven't seen anything yet. Come on. I will go in first, Avalon follow me and Nickolai follow her in. Okay?"

I nod.

Rob turns and walks into the gateway. Well, here goes nothing. I brace myself and walk into the silvery gateway to the new world that awaits me.

GLOSSARY

For all those pesky words you might not know how to pronounce or what they are.

Sidhe – (Shee) The name for the Otherworld and the people that live there.

Firbolg – (**feer**-buhl-*uh* g) The people that lived on Ireland before the Tuatha De Danann came.

Merrow – The Irish term for Mermaid, Merman or Siren.

Milesian – (Mi·le·sian) The last settlers of Ireland.

Tuatha De Danann – The supernatural race that settled in Ireland and fled to the Sidhe (Otherworld) and rule it to this day.

Samhain – (Sow-en) Irish gaelic word for Halloween.

ACKNOWLEDGEMENTS

I give thanks to my husband, for taking care of our home and children. He took care of everything while I was out tending to the imaginary people in my head.

Thank you to my kids, for putting up with mommy's absence.

Melinda Fowler and Brandon Clayton, my kickass proofreaders, thanks for helping me polish up the mess of a first draft I gave you.

Thanks to my friends at the Hangout, for keeping me sane. Bouncing ideas off you guys has been a God send.

DID YOU ENJOY THIS BOOK?
YOU CAN MAKE A BIG DIFFERENCE!

Reviews are the most valuable tools authors have when it comes to getting attention for their books.

You can help out in a big way! If you enjoyed this book, I would appreciate it if you would take five minutes to leave a review.

Amazon: https://www.amazon.com/gp/product/B00OJNJ7QC

GoodReads: https://www.goodreads.com/review/edit/25770436

I invite you to follow me on Facebook, Twitter, Instagram and my website. These are the best places to reach me and I would love to chat about the characters and books with you. I look forward to hearing from you. You can follow along with me on updates and things across all of my accounts.

http://juliescholfield.wordpress.com
http://facebook.com/JulieScholfieldBooks
http://twitter.com/JulieScholfield
http://instagram/julie.scholfield

Keep reading for a sneak peek at Altered, book two in the Otherworld Origins series.

CHAPTER 1

Avalon

The large, half-naked, tattooed man standing before me, wasn't what I expected to see when stepping into the gateway in Utah. The man appears to be in his late forties with grey hair sprinkled through his long, dark, braided hair. His face is covered with what looks like tribal markings in bluish-black ink. His markings continue down the rest of his body, covering his shoulders, arms and chest. The tattoos continue farther down pass his stomach and disappear into the waistband of his loose drawstring pants. I look up at his face and see that his eyes are wide and his mouth is open in what appears to be shock. I try to ignore his gaping stare and look at the new world that surrounds me.

Alder and birch trees surround the gateway we just finished entering through. The leaves on the trees are bright green and almost seem luminescent. The air is clean and free of the smells of modern civilization. Wild flowers are scattered haphazardly across the grass of the small space that Bain, Rob and now Nickolai stand in. I can't see any buildings or other structures not from nature here. It almost feels like we dumped ourselves into the middle of the woods with only the tattooed man as company.

I can feel the large man's eyes on me. I sigh and turn to face him again.

"What?" I ask, not hiding the fact that the stare is starting to tick me off. Don't the people here know that it is rude to stare?

The man looks at Rob with an expression on his face that reminds me of the actor, The Rock, but still does not say a word.

Rob nods to him and then the man abruptly falls onto one knee in front of me.

I look to Rob in shock. I have a feeling what this means.

"Okay, I didn't hear you say anything but from the looks of it, I'd say he knows. I thought we weren't going to be telling anyone just yet?" I ask.

"Bain does not come to court much, so the fact that he knows will not cause problems for us on our journey." Rob explains. "As to not saying anything, well, that is something I forgot to tell you about before."

"Tell me what?" I wait somewhat impatiently with my hands on my hips.

"That we can talk mind to mind with those that are near to fully Awakened." Rob blurts out.

"Fully Awakened? What does that mean? Why haven't you talked to me this way? It would have been helpful in the mine that is for sure." I reply.

"Well, you aren't fully Awakened yet." Rob says. "Not even close."

I look at Nickolai and he looks at me the confusion obvious on his face.

"How do you know I'm not?" I ask.

"Because I cannot speak to you mind to mind. I have a hard enough time just picking up your thoughts. Plus there is the whole change you never went through." Rob replies.

I thought that because I'm descended from two different Fae was the reason there wasn't much change?" I look over at Nickolai, who shrugs, and then look to Rob.

"We will discuss this more later. There will be plenty of time for you to get your questions answered and in detail by those that know more about your family. Right now, we need to get going." Rob turns to Bain, clasps his upper arm, and nods once before walking out of the enclosure of the trees.

It feels like I got dismissed. I don't like it. I look back at Nickolai for a moment, turn and run after Rob with Nickolai close behind me. I may not like what he just did, but I don't want to get left here either. I run pass the tree line and continue to where I think Rob went.

"Stop!" Rob's voice calls out. It's so loud it almost hurts my ears.

I stop abruptly and turn towards the sound of his voice. "Why were you hiding over there?" I ask Rob as Nickolai stops behind me.

"I was not hiding. If you go too much further, those trees will thin out. You will run straight off a cliff!" Rob walks closer to me and takes my hand. A look of concern and thoughtfulness crosses his face. "I thought you would be able to see where I went but I forgot that you cannot follow the trail that I leave yet."

"Trail?" I ask.

"Magical Trail. I know you will be able to see it once you are fully Awakened, if that is what you choose to do." Rob replies.

"Oh."

I didn't know what else to say. It seems there is more to being fully Awakened than he really wants to tell me. It almost feels as if he thinks I'd not want to should I know everything. It just makes me curious as to what the big secret is that could possibly change my mind.

"Come on, we have a ways to go, and without you being able to move as fast as Nickolai and myself, it is going to take at least a day to get to the palace." Rob motions for us to follow him as he slowly makes his way toward the direction of the trees.

The dense trees abruptly thin out and reveal a sharp drop off. The sun is shining brightly and the blue sky is dusted with light wispy clouds. A large forest spreads out in full view below the cliff. The trees look huge and I can only see the tops! Large birds circle above a section of the forest and dive down sporadically into the canopy. I can hear something off in the distance but I'm not sure what it is. I look over at Nickolai to ask him what he thinks the noise might be and find him staring out towards the forest.

"Is that where we are going?" Nickolai asks Rob as he points at something in the distance that I can't see.

"That is it. It will take another day to reach." Rob replies.

"What do you see?" I ask Nickolai.

"A tall gleaming white spire. I assume it's tall since its poking up above the treetops." Nickolai answers.

I walk closer to the edge of the cliff and take a look down. A low cloud seems to be hovering below, obscuring the ground underneath it. I turn to ask Rob about what we will find down there when the ground beneath my left foot crumbles. I scream as I start to fall.

ABOUT THE AUTHOR

Julie Scholfield was born in Stockton, California and fell in love with marine animals growing up near the Pacific Ocean. She currently lives in Northern Colorado. Julie loves to read fantasy novels, paint, and play with her kids.

Her first fantasy novel, Awakened was released on October 14th, 2014, the first of a series called Otherworld Origins. She is currently working on Altered, the second book of the , which is due out in the December of 2016!